The Collected

Thra>

Thraxas and
the Oracle

Martin Scott

Thraxas and the Oracle

In the tenth book of the series, armies are gathering. It's time for Thraxas and Makri to march back towards Turai. Lisutaris is War Leader and she trusts Thraxas enough to make him her personal security officer. Captain Thraxas is given the difficult task of outwitting Deeziz the Unseen, the enemy's most powerful sorcerer. He could do with some help from Makri. Unfortunately Makri spends most of her time hiding from the Elf with whom she once had an unsatisfactory relationship. Thraxas is relieved to meet a few familiar faces, refugees from Turai, but as he tries to prevent Deeziz from ruining the war effort, he finds himself baffled, outmanoeuvred, and badly in need of beer.

For more about Thraxas visit
www.thraxas.com
www.martinmillar.com

Cover Model: Madeline Rae Mason

Introduction to Thraxas Book Ten

It's time for Thraxas to march back towards Turai, in an army led by Lisutaris. When I started the series, I didn't envisage that Thraxas would ever be given an official position, but now he's a Captain. I didn't foresee that Lisutaris would become War Leader either, and I certainly didn't foresee that Makri would ever be welcomed into the army. These characters just seemed to grow into their positions.

Thraxas would prefer to be in the Avenging Axe with a flagon of ale, though at the moment, he's not certain if the Avenging Axe even exists any more. Makri is still determined to go to the University in Turai, even though that might also have been destroyed. If you're wondering if I have this all carefully planned out, I don't. At this moment I don't really know if the Avenging Axe still exists either. And if Makri ever does make it to the university, I don't know how she'll get on. I've never been a very good planner. I just start off with the characters and see where the stories go. That can lead to difficulties. A little more planning might not go amiss, actually.

Martin Millar

Thraxas and the Oracle

Chapter One

'You understand, Thraxas, that you'll have to remain sober? We can't have any repeat of your past behaviour.'

I'm puzzled by Lisutaris's words. She doesn't seem to be making sense. 'What exactly do you mean?'

'I think my meaning was quite clear. You are to remain sober at all times. We're about to embark on a desperate fight for survival and I don't want you rolling around in the gutter when you may be needed for vital work.'

I've been getting along with Lisutaris, Head of The Sorcerers Guild, rather better in recent times, but I don't like the sound of this.

'Firstly, Lisutaris, I do not "roll around in the gutter." I may quaff a flagon of ale every now and then, for relaxation. No one has ever accused me of taking it to excess–'

'Everyone has accused you of taking it to excess.'

'–secondly, I really don't see that my level of intoxication is going to be a deciding factor in the war against the Orcs.'

I might have added "thirdly, who the hell are you to tell me what I can do?" but as Lisutaris, Mistress of the Sky, has recently been appointed War Leader and is now the supreme Commander of the western armies, she does have a good claim on being able to tell people what to do, even me.

'Thraxas, I've just given you an extremely important position in my inner circle. I've promoted you to Captain, against the advice of everyone who's ever met you. So stop arguing, get ready for action, and stay sober.'

I could argue further. As a free Turanian citizen, I'm perfectly entitled to drink as much as I want. It's a matter of principle, even if all free Turanian citizens have been driven out of Turai. Our city

1

may have been conquered by the Orcs, but our laws remain. True, I am back in the army again, but that never stopped me before. Lisutaris halts any further discussion by raising her hand imperiously, something at which she's become adept since being appointed War Leader.   •

Now that the nations of the west have managed to assemble, the Elves have joined us from the south, and we're finally ready to march, I had been expecting to take my place in the army as a common foot-soldier. I'd planned to join up with one of the phalanxes of Turanian exiles. Despite my years of military experience, I've never been involved with the top ranks of the military. Generals have tended to ignore the talents of Thraxas of Turai. Lisutaris apparently feels differently. She summoned me to her headquarters and enlisted me on the spot. I'm now a Captain in the Sorcerers Auxiliary Regiment. Not just any old Captain either. I'm Chief Security Officer of the Commander's Personal Security Unit. I can announce myself as Captain Thraxas, CSO CPS. Captain Thraxas, CSO CPSU SAR if I feel like it. I was vaguely honoured, till she started lecturing me about staying sober.

Lisutaris turns to Makri, who escaped from Turai with us, floating west on a leaky fishing boat before finally washing up in Samsarina. 'You will remain as my bodyguard. I'm giving you the rank of Ensign in the Sorcerers Auxiliary Regiment. Like Thraxas you're part of the Commander's Personal Security unit. You'll answer only to me, but it does place you under military discipline. So keep your temper in check and obey my orders.'

So Makri has a title too, and responsibility, and letters after her name. Ensign Makri, BG CPSU SAR. I'm half expecting Makri to object. She's not a woman who enjoys taking orders. Strictly speaking, she's not a woman at all, with her Elvish and Orcish blood. However she accepts it calmly enough. Makri has acted as Lisutaris's bodyguard before. It's a little different now that she's actually been drafted into the army. Having her in uniform, so to speak, might help to allay some of the suspicions people have of her. Makri was born in the east and grew up in an Orcish gladiator pit. With her reddish skin and pointed ears, she does tend to arouse suspicion in the west, particularly here in Samsarina where they're

2

not used to anyone with Orcish blood. She's quite a well-known figure now, after her victory in the great sword-fighting tournament, but I'm not sure if the broad masses of Samsarinans are happy about her presence.

'Will I be in the front lines?' asks Makri.

'Unlikely. Not at first anyway. I'm War Leader. I need to plan, organise, and get this army in as good shape as possible. I can't go charging into combat first chance I get, much as I'd like to.'

Makri frowns. That's not what she was hoping to hear. 'But I want to fight.'

'You'll get your chance eventually. When the important fighting occurs, I'll be there with the rest of the sorcerers. However we won't be involved in the advance operations.'

Makri scowls. 'But I–'

'Enough, Ensign Makri.' Lisutaris holds up her hand again. 'I've no time to discuss it further. I have to talk to three ambassadors in five minutes and you're coming with me. Captain Thraxas, meet me at my command centre in one hour. Don't be late.'

'I still don't like this *staying sober* business.'

'And you'll both address me as Commander,' says Lisutaris. 'You're in the army now.'

The Head of the Sorcerers Guild sweeps out of the room, accompanied by a rather unhappy looking Makri. I exit swiftly myself. There's a tavern not far from here. Best get a few beers inside me while I still have the chance.

Chapter Two

North of the capital, east of the river, the Samsarinan plain stretches out for thirty miles or so before the land starts to rise towards the hilly region that separate Samsarina from Simnia. Mostly it's farmland, but for the moment much of it has been requisitioned by the King as a base. The military encampment is growing every day. The Samsarinan army is gathered in full force, and troops have been arriving from the smaller states in the south, like Hadassa and Namaste. There are a few more battalions from further west, though less than expected. That's a common problem. Preparations have gone fairly smoothly, but every allied army that's arrived has been smaller than hoped for. That includes the Elves. They've been making their way up from the Southern Isles in their long ships, but most islands are sending less than last time.

King Gardos of Samsarina can't wait much longer for late arrivals. Soon we'll be heading north-east to join up with the Simnian army, then on to meet the Niojans. Moving such vast forces, and keeping them supplied, presents many problems. The major western nations are used to it, however. Much of the logistical support is still in place from the last time we repelled an Orcish invasion, less than twenty years ago.

In the space between the long lines of military tents and the city walls, in a grove of trees now festooned with messages pinned onto boards, there's a gathering point for refugees, recruits, and all the displaced persons made homeless by the war. Mercenaries and northern barbarians arrive to join up with the army. Others search for lost relatives, or just a place to stay for a while. In amongst the confused mass of people there's a large, square tent over which flies a Turanian flag. Sitting at a table in front of the tent is an official from the remnants of the Turanian civil service, an ex-palace employee. He's keeping records of all survivors who've made it this far. The entire population of Turai is either dead or homeless, and refugees have been straggling into Samsarina all through the winter. Men of military age are assigned to the surviving Turanian regiments, and the others are housed as best as can be arranged.

4

I've known the Turanian official for a long time. His name's Dasinius. He was a senior scribe at the Imperial Palace back when I was employed there as an official investigator. We never liked each other. That doesn't seem to matter much any more. With our city taken by the Orcs, old feuds have lost their importance. As I approach, he shakes his head wearily. He knows why I'm here. Every day I've checked to see if there might be any sign of Gurd, or Tanrose, my old friends from the Avenging Axe. I don't have any particular hope of finding them alive. I was lucky to escape from the sack of Turai and there's no reason to be optimistic about anyone else's survival. Even so, I haven't given up hope. Gurd is a tough man. He wouldn't lay down his life easily. If he did manage to escape, it's not impossible that he'd end up here. Simnia is closer to the borders of Turai but Turanians have never got on well with Simnians. They'd be more likely to head for Samsarina, even if it mean a longer march through the winter landscape.

Finding no sign of my old friends, I head inside the city walls and get myself outside of two tankards of beer. Good beer, I have to say. With plenty of fine farmland, the Samsarinans know how to grow high-quality hops and barley. I consider taking a third, but control myself. Probably I shouldn't drink too much when I'm about to start my official duties with Lisutaris. Not on the same day she warned me about drinking too much anyway.

I make my way to her military headquarters, meanwhile musing on my unexpected promotion to Captain. I've been a soldier and a mercenary many times, but never an officer. The highest I rank I ever achieved was corporal in a phalanx, responsible for keeping my row of men in line. Despite my fighting experience, commanders never thought it appropriate to promote me further. Mostly down to class prejudice, I'd say. The blinkered aristocrats who get to be generals are rarely able to appreciate the finer qualities of a strong working man like myself.

'If they'd made me a General we probably wouldn't be in this mess right now. Maybe I'll get some respect now I'm a Captain.'

It's odd that Makri is now also in the military, with the rank of Ensign. Not an especially high rank, but prestigious in her case because she's the personal bodyguard of our War Leader. That's too important a position for anyone to dismiss lightly. For the first time in her life, Makri has a position which demands respect, even from people who are suspicious of her. It should make her life easier, though I don't expect it will re-assure everyone. Since she won the sword-fighting contest, I've heard whispers that she owes her fighting skill to some dread Orcish sorcery. It's rumoured she can talk to dragons, and called one down to help her win the contest. All nonsense of course, though understandable in a way. Her incredible fighting prowess is difficult for people to understand in any normal terms.

I call in at one of the supply depots set up around the city walls to pick up my military uniform. I hand over the signed authorisation from Lisutaris. The standard grey military tunic they give me has a flash of colour on the collar, a small rainbow with a sword laid over it.

'What's that?'

'Badge of the Sorcerers Auxiliary Regiment,' says the supply sergeant.

I'm scowling as I take the garment. Being a Captain is all very well, but in truth I'm not that keen on being in the Sorcerers Auxiliary Regiment. Most of their work involves protecting sorcerers on the battlefield. It's not so bad, I suppose, but it's not ideal. People have been known to mock the SAR for not being proper soldiers. People like me, for instance. I don't want to spend all my time shepherding hapless sorcerers around the place. It's not as if every sorcerer is a big asset in wartime. A powerful magic-user like Lisutaris is invaluable of course, when there are dragons pouring out of the sky, but I've seen young sorcerers arrive on the battlefield full of themselves one minute, before turning tail the next as they realise they're not up to the task.

I walk on, through the city gate, and along the road that leads to Lisutaris's headquarters. The road is busy with supply wagons, messengers and government officials. Such is the bustle that I'm surprised, on presenting myself at the mansion, to be shown straight in. With so much going on I'd have expected to wait. Waiting a long time for anything is standard in wartime.

A Samsarinan corporal leads me along a corridor and up a broad flight of stairs. He does address me as Captain, noting the rank on my sleeve, but I'm not certain he's as respectful as he should be. I'm shown into a waiting room and am once again surprised to be summoned right away. A young female sorcerer leads me through to a room where Lisutaris and Makri are standing in front of a large map, studying it intently. Lisutaris is draped in a plain grey cloak with the rainbow motif of the sorcerers guild embroidered discretely on each shoulder. Other than that, I can't see any indication of her rank. Makri is wearing armour which looks suspiciously like the light Orcish armour she wore back in Turai, skilfully wrought from chainmail and leather. I've no idea where she might have obtained it from. One might have thought it would be more tactful not to wear Orcish armour, given the circumstances, but Makri isn't known for her tact.

'Captain Thraxas,' says Lisutaris. 'Thanks for arriving promptly. And only drinking two flagons of ale.'

I don't know if that's just an accurate guess. Maybe she used some sort of spell.

'Are you ready to take up your duties?'

'Do I have to be in the Sorcerers Auxiliary Regiment?'

'What's wrong with the Sorcerers Auxiliary Regiment?'

'They're not renowned as warriors. And they have a foolish rainbow badge.' I glare at my epaulet.

'We have a serious problem,' says Lisutaris. Presumably she doesn't mean my rainbow badge. 'You remember Deeziz?'

'Of course.'

Deeziz the Unseen is the most powerful of the Orcish sorcerers. A few months ago she infiltrated Turai, undetected by either the city's intelligence services or our Sorcerers Guild. She outsmarted us completely. It was her actions that led to the fall of the city.

'I believe she may be headed this way.'

That does sound like a serious problem. I wouldn't mind a face-to-face encounter with Deeziz, because there are a lot of things I'd like to pay her back for, preferably with my sword, but it's not likely to happen that way. If she turns up in Samsarina it's going to be difficult to spot her. Deeziz moved into the Avenging Axe in

Turai, my home tavern, and was so well-disguised that even Lisutaris couldn't detect her. Her sorcery fooled everyone. She pretended to be a popular singer called Moolifi, and did it so well that poor Captain Rallee fell in love with her. When she turned out to be an Orcish sorcerer, it was quite a shock. We didn't have much time to dwell on it, as she swiftly brought down the north wall of Turai, allowing the Orcish army to march into the city.

Lisutaris is scowling. When Deeziz did finally reveal herself, she'd mocked Lisutaris for spending too much time at parties, squandering her power, while Deeziz herself had practiced and studied, increasing her own strength. The way things turned out, it was hard to argue with her.

'Deeziz the Unseen has by far the strongest powers of concealment I've ever encountered,' continues Lisutaris. 'No one had an inkling she was in our midst. Even Horm the Dead was fooled. In the past weeks I've made efforts to develop my detection spells. I saw her aura that day in the tavern, and there's a chance I'd recognise it again. Since we arrived in Samsarina I've been looking east for traces of her. Two days ago I thought I sensed something. It was the merest flicker, for a fraction of a second. I could be wrong, but…'

'But she could be riding into town disguised as a tavern girl?'

'Indeed. Her powers of concealment are so strong I'm not even sure she'd have to remain female. She might be able to take on the form of a man and join up with the army, or the mercenaries.'

We fall silent for a moment. There's no need to stress the damage it could do if the most powerful Orcish sorcerer is allowed to operate undetected in our midst.

'I'll keep working on detection spells. I can't devote as much time to that as I'd like, with all my other responsibilities, but I've instructed several other sorcerers to work on it as well. Meanwhile I want you to take this in hand, Thraxas. I've made you my head of security. If Deeziz the Unseen arrives, find her.'

'That sounds almost impossible.'

'I know. But I need you to do it.'

I nod my head. 'I'll think of something.'

'If Deeziz attempts to infiltrate the army - or to assassinate me, another possibility - she might not be alone. Even for a woman as powerful as her, there has to be a lot of risk involved in straying so far from home, among so many enemies. I wonder if she might have some support. A network of agents, to provide her with shelter, perhaps. At the very least, I'd think she'd require another agent to send messages back to the Orcs. I doubt she'd risk sorcerous transmission herself. Our own sorcerers are checking for that sort of thing constantly.'

'Do you have any means of identifying her? If I find a likely suspect is there some sorcerous test that will expose her?'

Lisutaris shakes her head. 'Not so far. My new Sorcerous Detection Unit is trying to develop a more advanced spell that might work.'

'Who's in this unit?'

'Irith Victorious from Juval, and two of his guild. Do you know him?'

'I knew him a long time ago. I met him again at the sorcerers Assemblage.'

I'm troubled to hear Irith's name, though I don't let it show. I first met him when I was a young soldier, fighting in the south. When he appeared in Turai at the sorcerers Assemblage, a few years ago, we did a lot of drinking together. Then I robbed him when he was drunk. I was obliged to steal some information that was vital for our city. I didn't feel very good about it at the time. I don't know if he ever learned about it. He probably did.

'They're working in secret so don't mention them to anyone. They haven't come up with anything yet but I'm hopeful. Meanwhile you'll just have to manage without magical assistance.'

'It's going to involve a lot of trekking round, looking for suspicious characters. I could use some help.'

'I'll be assigning you staff,' says Lisutaris. 'Meanwhile, I've asked someone else to assist.'

Lisutaris snaps her fingers, causing an internal door to fly open. A small dark-clad figure walks silently into the room.

'Hanama?' I make no effort to hide my displeasure.

'Captain Hanama. New Chief Intelligence Officer of the Commander's Personal Security Unit.'

'Captain? Chief Intelligence Officer? You do realise she's an assassin?'

'Not relevant in the circumstances, Thraxas.'

'Not relevant? She kills people for money.'

'Well, we are soldiers,' says Makri. 'You could say that about all of us.'

'It's not the same! Why are you employing her? Are you sure she's even on our side?'

I glare at Hanama. She's quite a small woman, with short dark hair. She looks very young and her skin is very pale. Probably from spending most of her time sneaking round at night, assassinating people.

'Of all the people I'd hoped escaped from the wreck of Turai, you weren't one of them.'

Hanama doesn't deign to reply.

'How did you get here?' I demand.

'I walked.'

'You should have kept on walking.'

'Enough!' says Lisutaris. 'I trust Hanama and that should be good enough for you. As Chief Security Officer and Chief Intelligence Officer you'll work together, without argument, or I'll have something to say about it.'

I wish I'd had another beer. Hanama, number three in the Turanian Assassins Guild - maybe higher these days for all I know - right at the heart of the war effort. I can't believe it's a good idea.

'I should get started right away,' I say. Partly because I'm keen to get started right away, and partly because I'm annoyed to find myself in the same room as Hanama.

'Good. I'm assigning Anumaris Thunderbolt to your security staff. You know her, I believe?'

Anumaris Thunderbolt walks into the room on cue. She's young, recently qualified and without much experience. Even so, I'm reasonably pleased to see her, because I did encounter her on the battlefield outside Turai. For a young sorcerer, she did well. Didn't lose her head, and fired a few powerful spells at the Orcs.

Surrounded by Lisutaris, Makri, Hanama and Anumaris, I feel like asking Lisutaris if she's planning on recruiting any actual men to fight the war, but I hold my tongue. Anumaris tells me that there's an office upstairs we can use until the army marches. I follow her out. In the corridor outside there are a group of fair-haired Elves waiting to see Lisutaris. None I recognise, though from their clothing and insignia they're important figures. Even if their numbers are fewer than we'd hoped for, it's a relief to see the Elves. Without them we'd have no chance of defeating Prince Amrag and his Orcish horde.

I climb the stairs with Anumaris. 'It will be exciting going into battle with Elves,' she says.

I nod. I wouldn't call it exciting, but it's re-assuring. 'They're more reliable than some of the lowlifes I've found myself sharing a phalanx with, anyway.'

'Lowlifes?'

'Turanian phalanxes weren't made up of the cream of society. Dregs of the earth, half of them. They'd have collapsed in battle without a man like me in the middle, supporting everyone else.'

'I see...'

'If it wasn't for me the Turanian infantry would have crumbled years ago. Turai too, I expect. Is this our office? Isn't there somewhere bigger?'

'It's only for a short while, till we march north.'

I look around. I'm not very impressed. 'Where's the couch?'

'There's a chair. Won't that do?'

I look sternly at Anumaris Thunderbolt. 'A chair? Anumaris, what rank are you?'

'Storm Class sorcerer, Sorcerers Regiment.'

I've no idea what Storm Class means. I let it pass. 'Well, Storm Class sorcerer Anumaris, if you're going to be working in my security unit, there's some things you need to know right from the start. Most importantly, your chief officer needs a couch. I can't sleep properly in a chair. Find me a couch.'

Young Anumaris looks perplexed. 'Surely you won't be sleeping in your office?'

'Of course I will. The ability to sleep in difficult circumstances has carried me through more campaigns than you'll ever see.'

'But what about when we're on the march? Out in the field?'

'We'll improvise. Or rather, you will. You're a sorcerer. I expect you to be able to produce a couch when necessary.'

'I'll do my best.'

'Good. Stick with me and I'll get you through this war. Lisutaris said she was assigning me staff. Where are they?'

'It's just me so far.'

'Really? Well, you'll have to do, I suppose. As well as a couch, I need beer.'

Anumaris screws up her face and looks uncomfortable. 'I'm not allowed to bring you beer. Orders from Lisutaris.'

I stare at her suspiciously. 'Lisutaris, Mistress of the Sky, War Leader and supreme commander of the forces of the west, specifically instructed you not to bring me beer?'

'Yes.'

'Really?'

'Yes.'

'Very strange. You'd think she'd have better things to do. Like organising armies. It hardly inspires confidence.'

Anumaris doesn't reply. I get the impression that's she's someone who will not lightly ignore orders from out War Leader. That could become irritating. I notice her rainbow cloak is in good condition. So are the rest of her clothes. She doesn't look like a young woman who's gone through many hardships recently.

'How did you fight your way out of Turai?'

'I didn't,' she admits. 'I was outside the city walls when the Orcs attacked. I'd been visiting my parents on their farm. I tried going back but it was hopeless. All the refugees told me the city had fallen. So I headed west, looking for other sorcerers. That's what we've been trained to do.'

'I see. I had to fight my way out in a bloody struggle, rescuing Lisutaris and Makri at the same time. After that I navigated our way here on a leaky old boat and helped establish Lisutaris as War Leader. Remember that next time you start criticising me about couches and beer.'

I try the chair for size. It's not satisfactory. Not built for a man of my size. 'Were there any other Turanian sorcerers with you?'

Anumaris shakes her head. 'No. And hardly any have shown up here.'

That's bad news, both for the war effort and for the City-State of Turai. Turai is small in comparison to many of our neighbours, but we've always had plenty of sorcerers. Our superior magic has protected us.

'Perhaps we'll find some when we meet up with the Simnians. They might be waiting for us.' I rise to my feet. 'Now, about Deeziz the Unseen. We need to find her.'

'Where will we start?'

'The nearest tavern.'

Anumaris looks concerned. 'You're really not supposed to—'

'Don't you know anything about military discipline? We're not going to get very far if you start arguing every time I issue an order. Deeziz's last appearance in a human city was in the Avenging Axe, a tavern. Prior to that she'd been working as a singer in a theatre, also a popular drinking haunt. So it's quite likely that if she's arrived here, we'll find her somewhere similar. We'll start at the local taverns and work our way outwards. Does this office have any funds?'

'There's a safe in that wall. I'm not sure how much is in it.'

'Do you have the spell to open it?'

'Yes.'

'Then gather up the money and follow me. You're about to get your first lesson in security work.'

13

Chapter Three

We're in the wealthy part of town where there are mansions, villas and temples. We have to walk a few streets south before we come to a tavern. Anumaris hesitates.

'What's the matter? Haven't you ever been in a tavern before?'

She shakes her head.

'Never?'

'No.'

'How old are you?'

'Twenty-two.'

I'm astonished. I hardly know what to say. Twenty-two years old and never been in a tavern? My first thought is that she might be suffering from some sort of mental deficiency. A fear of crowds, perhaps. However she joined the Sorcerers Regiment, so she can't be all that scared of company. Perhaps her parents didn't approve of her visiting Turai's many drinking haunts. Young Anumaris is rather well-spoken. Not an aristocrat, but a daughter of the land-owning gentry. No doubt they were a respectable family. She looks very dubiously at the sign above the door. *The King's Shield.*

'Is it safe?'

'Safe? How sheltered has your life been?'

'Not sheltered at all!' Anumaris is offended. 'I just haven't had occasion to visit taverns. I grew up on the family estate. Then I went to sorcerers college. Everyone considered that quite daring.'

I'm about to let go with some hearty criticism of her, her family estate, and sorcerers college, but I restrain myself. She did appear on the battlefield outside Turai, after all, and stood up to the enemy attack when plenty of others crumbled. She must have something about her.

'Enough discussion.' I open the door and march inside. The young sorcerer follows me in. The tavern is crowded and noisy, the same as every other tavern in Samsarina, with mercenaries and off-duty soldiers taking the opportunity for some last minute revelry before we march off to war. There's a contingent of market workers close to the bar. I'm obliged to use my body-weight to force my way through, pulling Anumaris behind me.

'You see that? Take that as your first lesson in investigation. When there's a crowd in front of you, preventing you from reaching the bar, there's no point messing around asking them politely to step out the way. It'll get you nowhere. Just look for their weak spot and force your way through.

'What does that have to do with investigation?'

'Haven't you been listening to anything I've said? A tavern is the best place for gathering information. Whatever's going on in a city you'll find out about it here. Back in Turai I sometimes had to visit seven or eight in a day. Barmaid, two tankards of ale please.'

'Could I have a glass of water?' says Anumaris.

'Only if you want to mark yourself out as a hopeless outsider who will never be any good at security work, thereby letting down the armies of the west and probably leading to our ultimate defeat. Now take this tankard and try not to look like someone who grew up riding ponies in a frilly dress.'

Anumaris Thunderbolt scowls at me. She sips the ale, and makes a face.

'Once you've got that inside you you'll be half-way to making a decent investigator.'

'But Lisutaris said—'

'Enough about Lisutaris. There's no need to talk about her continually. She has her job to do and we have ours.'

'I really don't see what we're doing here!'

'We're looking for anything strange. Just keep your eyes and ears open. If we don't come across anything untoward, we'll move on to the next tavern.' I scan the crowd. 'When Deeziz the Unseen came to Turai, she disguised herself as a popular singer called Moolifi. I'll be interested to learn if any foreign singers have arrived in Samsarina recently.'

'Surely she wouldn't try the same thing again?'

'Probably not, but it's all we have to go on.'

Anumaris is dissatisfied. 'Deeziz could disguise herself as a tavern worker, or a market vendor. Any woman at all. Lisutaris thinks she might even be able to disguise herself as a man. How can we possibly find her? It seems hopeless.'

15

I drink down a good portion of ale. 'Investigations often seem hopeless at first. That doesn't mean you don't make a start. You do what you can, and keep going till something turns up. Maybe we'll get lucky. Maybe Deeziz will make a mistake. Maybe Lisutaris's sorcerers will come up with something. Either way, we keep on trying.'

Anumaris seems reasonably impressed by my little speech. It doesn't prevent her from looking at me disapprovingly when I grab a second beer from the bar. I tell her to stop complaining.

'I wasn't complaining.'

'You were thinking about it. Save your anti-beer fanaticism for some other time. And try engaging in some conversation with people. We're here to gather information.'

'I'm not very good at talking to strangers.'

'Then you'll have a fantastic career as an investigator. If you can't talk to anyone, listen to me, and learn how it's done.'

I've never had any problem talking to strangers. Mostly I've made my living from it. At this moment, in this tavern, it's easier than usual because of my Captain's insignia, which does grant me a degree of respect. It's obvious to everyone that I'm not one of those officers who's been promoted due to family connections. I'm a man who's seen plenty of combat. Hardened in battle, I like to think. I talk to soldiers, mercenaries, barmaids and traders, mostly about the approaching war. I learn a lot about the hopes and fears of the population though nothing that points to anything unusual. I have a feeling that if Deeziz the Unseen has arrived in Samsarina, there should already be some sign of her presence. What that sign might be, I don't know, and I don't pick up on anything.

I do notice that the mood is reasonably optimistic, even though everyone knows we're in for a tough campaign. Prince Amrag's reputation as a military commander has spread throughout the west. He's hated, like any Orcish leader, but people aren't making the mistake of dismissing his talents. He's got his Orcish phalanxes well organised and his cavalry well trained. The various Orcish nations are displaying more unity and discipline than they ever have before. Not only that, the Orcish Sorcerers Guild's control of dragons is more fearsome than ever. When you consider that our army won't be as large as we'd hoped, you might wonder why there's any optimism around. Partly it's because the Elves have arrived, and they have a very high reputation. Partly it's because for most people the war hasn't really started yet. Samsarina, Simnia and Nioj have yet to suffer casualties. Before their armies march out, it's easy for people to imagine everything going well, with a swift victory and a glorious return. It rarely works out that way.

'Or perhaps it just because we're in a tavern and everyone is full of beer,' I mutter to myself. For Turanians, the war started some time ago, and it hasn't gone well. I think about all the friends and comrades I've lost. I feel my mood worsening.

In the second tavern we visit, Anumaris Thunderbolt flatly refuses to drink any more alcohol. She asks the barmaid for a glass of water, which causes some mockery to which I don't take too kindly. I'm still sensitive about being placed in the Sorcerers Auxiliary Regiment. They don't have a great reputation for fighting or drinking.

'Are you trying to humiliate me?'

'What do you mean?'

'Drinking water is making the Sorcerers Auxiliary Regiment look bad.'

'That doesn't make sense,' says Anumaris. 'Anyway, I'm not in the SAR. I'm in the Sorcerers Regiment.'

'Even worse,' I mutter. 'Let's find another tavern.'

'I really think–'

'I've had enough of you thinking. When we get back I'm going to ask Lisutaris for some staff who aren't hopeless young prigs with no experience of war or drinking. If she expects me to babysit you through this campaign she's greatly mistaken.'

The young sorcerer looks hurt. I ignore her and march out through the door. In the street outside I bump into a brawny grey-haired barbarian. I'm about to tell him to watch where he's going when he suddenly cries out.

'Thraxas!'

'Gurd!'

I can't believe it. Gurd, my oldest companion, still alive.

'Gurd! I thought you were dead!'

17

'Me? No Orc is getting the better of me.'

'Where's Tanrose?'

'She's here too.'

The news that Tanrose, finest cook in Twelve Seas, escaped the wreckage of Turai, brings unaccustomed joy to my heart. Her unmatched stew and pie-making skills were one of the few things that made life in Turai worth living. I'm moved to embrace Gurd. I can't remember the last time I embraced anyone.

'I thought I'd find you here, you dog,' he roars, and pounds me on the back. 'Have you joined the Turanian regiment?'

'No, I'm with Lisutaris. Important work for the War Leader!'

'Can it wait?'

'Of course,' I cry. 'We need to find a tavern.' I turn to Anumaris. 'Investigating is finished for the day. I need to talk to Gurd.'

'I don't think—'

'No one cares what you think,' I tell her curtly. Then I give Gurd another hearty clap on the shoulder and we go off in search of a tavern to celebrate our joint survival, and catch up with each other's news. Finding Gurd alive is the only good thing that's happened in a long time.

Chapter Four

Later, well-ensconced at a corner table in the Beery Knave, a small, dark tavern in a small, dark alleyway, I'm toasting Gurd and Tanrose's survival with a large tankard of ale. He informs me he's only been in the city for two days.

'We're living in a tent up at the refugee camp, north of the walls. Not as bad as it sounds. they've got it well organised. Everyone who's fit and able gets the chance to join up with the army. I'll be doing that tomorrow.'

'How did you get out of Turai? When Deeziz worked that spell I blacked out. When I came round there was no one left in the Avenging Axe except Lisutaris and Makri. I dragged them out of there just before we were overrun. Had a close thing on the beach with a dragon.'

Gurd nods. 'I blacked out too. I was already sick with the winter malady. When I came round I was out in the street with Tanrose and a few others. I hardly knew what was going on. That Orcish sorcerer really fooled us all. I was standing there wondering what was happening when a squadron of Orcs came round the corner with pikes and shields. I took out my sword and got ready for my death stand.'

Gurd bangs his fist on the table. 'It would have been a good death stand! I'd have taken plenty of them with me.' He laughs. 'But I'd have died soon enough. I could hardly stay on my feet, with the illness and the sorcery. Tanrose would have died too.'

'So what happened?'

'Tirini saved us.'

'Tirini Snake Smiter?'

'That's right. You remember she was in the tavern too, for the big card game? She hobbled up, still dazed like everyone else, and still wearing her fur cloak and these fancy shoes. Could hardly walk. But she saved us all right. I tell you Thraxas, I'd no idea that woman was such a powerful sorcerer. She waved her arm and shouted out some spell. Next thing I knew we were all outside the city walls, quite a long way west. We could see the city burning but there were no Orcs or Dragons anywhere near.'

I raise my eyebrows. 'Tirini did that?'

'She did. Took me and Tanrose and two or three others with her. Just plucked us up and set us down about a mile away. It only seemed to take a few seconds. Strangest thing that's ever happened to me. '

I'm impressed, and surprised. Lisutaris does insist that Tirini Snake Smiter is a powerful sorcerer, though you wouldn't think that if you only knew her by reputation. With her perfectly dyed blonde hair, her extravagant make up, her expensive fancy clothes and so on, she's always seemed keener on fashion and scandalous relationships than practising sorcery. She featured regularly in the gossip sheets that circulated in Turai. She was denounced from the pulpit on more than one occasion by Archbishop Gzekius, who regarded her as the epitome of Turai's decadent and impious upper-classes. Decadent and impious she may be, but moving a group of people instantly through space is an extremely difficult thing to do. I presume she somehow opened a portal into the magic space and dragged everyone through. It's hard enough for a powerful sorcerer to do that for themselves. Taking a group of people with you would need sorcery of a very high level, higher than I thought she had.

'I didn't realise Tirini had so much power.'

Gurd nods, but looks troubled. 'She certainly saved our lives. But it cost her.'

'What do you mean?'

'It seemed like using such a powerful spell broke her mind, or something like that. Afterwards she couldn't speak. She could hardly walk, and it wasn't just the fancy shoes holding her back. It was like she'd used up every bit of her strength and had nothing left. I had to carry her. Eventually we found a horse and cart and we set off in that. We thought Tirini would get better but she didn't. After a day or two I was over the Winter Malady and we were all in reasonable shape, except for Tirini. She still hasn't recovered. She didn't speak for the whole journey. Could hardly get her to eat anything either.'

I nod my head. 'Instant travel through the magic space is dangerous as well as difficult. Sorcerers rarely risk it.'

20

Gurd frowns. 'I don't like it, Thraxas. I don't like that she saved us at such a cost to herself. You'd hardly recognise her if you saw her.'

'Where is she?'

'Tanrose is taking her to Lisutaris. Maybe she can help. Though I gather it's not easy to see Lisutaris these days, now she's War Leader.'

'Don't worry, Lisutaris will help. Tirini was her best friend.'

'I hope so. We met another Turanian sorcerer on the way here, but he wasn't much help.'

'Who was it?'

'Coranius. I didn't take to him.'

'Coranius the Grinder? That's good news, Gurd. He's got a lot of power, he'll be a help in the war.'

'Maybe, but he's a miserable man. Hardly spoke to us on the journey. Didn't help Tirini either. Seemed to think she should just pull herself together.'

A waitress plants a bowl of stew on the table. I thank her, give her a goodly tip, and start mashing up a few yams.

'So here we are, off to war again.'

Gurd nods. He's a large, brawny man, with huge arm muscles and long hair now mostly grey, still looking as barbaric as the day he appeared in Turai, which must be more than twenty years ago. We've fought as mercenaries and soldiers together many times. He ended up owning a tavern and I ended up as his tenant, which probably says something about which one of us is the wisest.

'What's this about you being in some private security unit? I was expecting you to be in the Turanian phalanxes with me.'

'I'd much rather be there. Unfortunately I've saved Lisutaris's life so many times she can't do without me. I tell you Gurd, without me looking after Lisutaris we'd have lost the war already.'

Gurd laughs. 'You saved her life? Are you sure it wasn't Makri?'

'Makri? She's been hopeless from the start. Absolutely useless. If I hadn't dragged her skinny frame onto that boat she'd be dragon food by now. Not that she was grateful. I tell you Gurd, the last few weeks have been a nightmare, shepherding these two women around.'

I bang my tankard on the table. 'You'd think a powerful sorcerer and a so-called champion gladiator might have been able to do something for themselves, but really they just left everything to me. They spent most of the time crying.'

'Crying?'

'Yes. Completely sickening. You know what Makri's like - always bragging about what a tough gladiator she was, and how many fights she won. Let me tell you that when something goes wrong, she still bursts into tears. Since Turai fell, she's spent most of the time sobbing like a baby. And Lisutaris is no better. You hear her talking about bringing down dragons, but given the slightest excuse, she'll burst into tears as well.'

Gurd looks shocked. 'Lisutaris too?'

'I swear it's true. I tell you Gurd, there were times when it was all I could do to stay sane, with Lisutaris wailing, and Makri blubbering away beside her. You know I can't stand it when women cry.'

'No one can.'

I give Gurd a stern look. 'You're not thinking of bursting into tears now we've met again, are you?'

'Certainly not.'

Having safely established that neither of us are going to cry, we get down to some drinking. I can't describe what a relief it is to see him alive. We're still swapping stories when Gurd announces that he has to leave. He's promised to meet Tanrose to buy supplies to take back to their tent. I'm disappointed.

'Can't she manage on her own?'

'I promised I'd be there.'

Unlike me, Gurd is a man who keeps his promises, even when he'd rather be downing ale. I should probably admire him for it. I grumble a little as he departs, and have myself another beer to make up for my disappointment. I look down at my empty bowl of stew. Not bad quality. Nothing like Tanrose could make, of course. I look around the small tavern, vaguely wondering what I should be doing next. Investigating, I suppose. But there's really nothing to investigate. Nothing I can think of anyway. If Deeziz the Unseen has arrived in Samsarina, I doubt she's going to reveal herself in the Beery Knave. I start to feel a little annoyed. It's all very well Lisutaris telling me to go out and find Deeziz, but isn't that something the sorcerers should be doing? I did once have a few sorcerous powers but they've mostly gone now. Nothing I can do is going to magically locate Deeziz. What was it I said To Anumaris Thunderbolt about just plodding round, looking for clues? I can't remember. Some nonsense, I expect.

'To hell with them all,' I mutter. 'Particularly Anumaris. I never thought the day would come when I'd be in a tavern with someone who asked for a glass of water. What was Lisutaris doing, putting her on my staff? If that's the best young sorcerer we've got, the west is doomed.'

I'm yawning. I should sleep. Since arriving in the capital I've been billeted in a barracks on the west of the city but it's a long way back there. I decide to head back to my new office at Lisutaris's headquarters and sleep there. I remember there isn't a couch. I told Anumaris to sort that out for me but I doubt if she has. Where is she anyway? Shouldn't she be around? I'll have something to say to her about deserting me when we're meant to be on duty.

Spring has arrived and it's a warm say in the Samsarinan capital. I give a cheerful wave to a squadron of heavily armed Elves who march by in good formation. I'm still yawning as I climb the stairs and enter my office. Inside is Anumaris Thunderbolt. The young sorcerer doesn't look that pleased to see me.

'Where did you get to?' I demand. 'You don't just wander off when you're on duty.'

'You told me to go away!'

'No I didn't.'

'Yes you did! You were extremely rude.'

I scowl at her. 'This is war. What do you expect? A pat on the back from the ladies sewing circle? My security department is a tough fighting unit. If you can't take it, go work somewhere else.'

'Your tough fighting unit seems to spend all its time drinking in taverns.'

'You mean *investigating* in taverns. And shouldn't you be addressing me as General? This is the army, show some discipline.'

'You're not a General. You're a Captain.'

'Are you sure?'

'Quite sure.'

'Very well. Captain it is. Now go away, I need to rest.' Suddenly I bump my leg on an unexpectedly large piece of furniture. 'What's this?'

'A couch. Sort of.'

'What do you mean sort of? Is it a couch or isn't it?'

'There aren't any couches available for requisition. I took four chairs and joined them up with a spell.'

I take a look at her handiwork. Four chairs, reasonably comfy, lined up and fixed together. Quite clever, really.

'Not bad. It's time you did something useful round here. The rest of your work has been a great disappointment.'

With that, I lie down on my new couch and fall asleep. My first day as Lisutaris's Chief Security Officer has been quite arduous, and I need my rest.

Chapter Five

The makeshift couch proves satisfactory but I don't manage to rest as long as I'd like. After what seems like a very short time I'm shaken awake by Anumaris. I glare at her angrily.

'Didn't I instruct you I wasn't to be disturbed?'

'No.'

'Well I meant to. Go away.'

'Commander Lisutaris is holding a meeting and you're to go there immediately.'

'Dammit. What does she want?'

'To conduct the war, I suppose,' says Anumaris with what may be a touch of sarcasm.

I haul myself to my feet, a little unsteadily.

'You can't go there looking like that,' says Anumaris.

'Like what?'

'Like a man who's just crawled out of a tavern after ten flagons of ale.'

'Was it ten?'

'I don't know! I was just guessing.'

'It's probably accurate enough.'

'You stink of alcohol. Lisutaris specifically ordered you not to drink! And she told me to make sure you didn't! You couldn't even make it through one day.'

The young sorcerer seems rather agitated by all this. Quite unexpectedly, she points at me and speaks a few arcane words. I feel a sudden chill, and shiver.

'What was that? Did you just work a spell on me?'

'Yes. The minor tidying spell. Now you don't smell of ale any more. And you look a bit neater. It will get you through the meeting.'

I'm sure it's against army discipline for your subordinated to suddenly fire spells at you. On the other hand, it's probably not such a bad thing. No point giving Lisutaris something to complain about.

'All right, let's go.'

'I don't think I'm invited,' says Anumaris.

'You're coming as my assistant. Pay attention to everything in case I need you to repeat it later.'

In the short time since she was chosen as War Leader, Lisutaris, Mistress of the Sky, has efficiently organised her command structure. At the centre are just four people. Herself, as overall commander and senior sorcerer, General Hemistos as infantry commander, Bishop-General Ritari as cavalry commander, and Lord Kalith-ar-Yil as Elvish commander. These appointments are both practical and political. Each officer has a good reputation and plenty of experience of fighting, and between them they represent most of the troops who'll make up the armies of the west. Hemistos is Samsarinan. Ritari is Niojan. We haven't joined up with the Niojan army yet but Lisutaris summoned him early, wanting the Niojans to know that they had a senior man in an important position. Lord Kalith-ar-Yil, whom I've encountered previously, is the most senior Elf in attendance, and has the loyalty of all the southern Elvish Isles.

There is one important nation missing from Lisutaris's central command. As yet no there's representative from Simnia. That could be a problem. Simnia has never liked Turai, and might be expected to chafe about a Turanian being War Leader. They'll complain more if they feel they're not represented at the heart of the command structure. I don't know what Lisutaris plans to do about that. Whatever happens, Lisutaris's position as War Leader seems secure. The young King of Samsarina supports her. The Elves wouldn't support anyone else. The Niojans aren't thought to be particularly happy about the appointment, particularly as Lisutaris is female, but they seem to have accepted the reality that there was no other candidate who could command enough support.

Beneath these central leadership figures are a number of other commanders. They have responsibility for important matters such as the fleet, which will be sailing along the coast, ready to support us when our route brings us closer to the sea. Then there's the commander with responsibility for provisions, another in charge of armaments, and another in charge of heavy equipment, our mounted crossbows and siege equipment and so on. It's not as large a group as I might have expected, and from what I've seen,

Lisutaris has things under tight control. She glances at me as I enter the room. 'Captain Thraxas,' she murmurs.

'Commander Lisutaris,' I reply, politely. All the aforementioned senior officers are here, as is Makri. Makri is admitted to all but the most secret meetings between the commanders. That's quite a turnaround in fortune for the ragged, uncivilised gladiator who arrived in Turai only a few years ago, with no notion of how to behave in polite society. She could hardly use cutlery. It was fortunate for her that she ran into me. I taught her most of what she knows these days.

We listen while General Mexes, a Samsarinan in charge of armaments, gives a report on the number of spears, swords and shields now available to the army. It's brief and to the point, as is the Elvish Admiral Arith's summary of our naval strength. I'm generally impressed. Arrangements for moving and provisioning the large army seem to be going smoothly. It says a lot for Lisutaris's powers of organisation and delegation. When each commander has made their report, Lisutaris declares herself satisfied. 'We'll set off in twenty four hours. We should meet up with the Simnian army in six days.'

I'm not called on to speak during the meeting. Lisutaris hasn't made it widely known that she suspects Deeziz the Unseen might be attempting to infiltrate our forces. My work has so far been carried out in secrecy I presume that's why she asks me stay behind when everyone else is dismissed.

'Storm Class Anumaris, stay behind as well.'

When the assorted commanders file out I'm left with Lisutaris, Anumaris and Makri. Lisutaris looks at me for a moment, then turns to Anumaris.

'Nice tidying spell. You've almost made Thraxas presentable.'

'There was really no need for it,' I protest.

Lisutaris apparently has other things on her mind because she doesn't pursue it. She hesitates for a few moment. 'Thraxas, I'm going to need your help with a delicate matter. This mustn't be spoken of to anyone else, is that clear?'

'Of course.' I wonder what sort of trouble Lisutaris has got herself into. Probably thazis-related. Lisutaris is a very heavy user of the drug and it's caused problems before. I have noticed she's been smoking less since becoming War Leader but it wouldn't surprise me if she'd run out of the illegal substance and needed me to find some more.

'Have you heard of the Vitin Oracle?'

'Yes. Used to be a famous place, back when people consulted oracles. Before the True Church declared they were all sacrilegious.'

Lisutaris lights a small stick of thazis. A flicker of disapproval flickers over Anumaris's face but disappears quickly.

'Some people still consult the oracles,' says Lisutaris. 'Even though the church condemned them.'

The True Church, dominant religion in the west, doesn't like oracles. I don't really know why. Probably because they had their roots in earlier religions. Anyway, they forbid their followers from consulting them. They have done for at least eighty years, and as the True Church has a lot of power, the oracles have mostly faded away. The Vitin Oracle, sacred to the Goddess Vitina, was the most famous.

'We'll be passing quite close to the Vitin Oracle just before we meet the Simnian army,' continues Lisutaris. 'A few of my senior sorcerers would like to consult it. Obviously, it's something that would have to be kept private. The True Church wouldn't approve. That might create problems, particularly with Nioj.'

I'm sure it would. Niojans are all religious fanatics. Though we're not due to meet up with their army for some days, their senior Commander, Bishop-General Ritari, is already here, along with Legate Apiroi, another high ranking diplomat. If they got wind of such a visit, there would be trouble. Angry messages would be sent back to their king, Lamachus, and there's no telling what might happen then. It's not only Nioj we'd have to worry about. The True Church doesn't hold as much sway in other nations, but it is influential. Too influential for our War Leader to offend at a time like this.

'Why do your sorcerers want to consult this oracle?' asks Makri, speaking for the first time. 'Do they believe in it?'

'Well…' Lisutaris makes a depreciating gesture with her hand. 'Not really. It's more of a tradition. A sort of leftover from older times. The Sorcerers Guild did used to be quite strongly identified with the Goddess Vitina and her oracle. Sorcery's roots still run deep into the past. There are a few members of the Guild who still hold a passing interest in the old religion.'

I've been waiting my turn to speak. 'When you say "A few members of the Guild still hold a passing interest in the old religion," might it be more accurate to say that the Sorcerers Guild actually contains a large, well-organised group of devotees, including yourself?'

Our War Leader looks alarmed. 'I wouldn't put it like that.'

'Really? Even though you secretly led a delegation to the Oracle right after you were elected as Head of the Guild? A delegation which included young Anumaris here who, I notice, isn't looking very surprised.'

Lisutaris's eyes blaze. 'How can you possibly know that?'

'I've been in your mansion in Turai. You shouldn't leave private correspondence to other sorcerers lying about. Not on sensitive matters anyway.'

'I never left any private correspondence lying about!'

'Well you shouldn't leave it in easily-accessible drawers.'

'How dare you examine the contents of my private desk!'

'I'm an investigator. I get curious. Particularly when I'm kept waiting for hours because you're busy doing your hair.'

Lisutaris shows signs of imminent eruption. Fortunately for me, she controls it, and lights another thazis stick instead.

'Is this true?' asks Makri.

'It is. And if it were known it would bring Lisutaris and the rest of her Guild into conflict with every church and bishop in the Western World.'

Lisutaris sighs. 'Most of them, I suppose. They do tend to be intolerant. Especially the Niojans. Bishop-General Ritari would be down on me like a bad spell if he learned I was off to consult the oracle. The Niojans would probably withdraw their support from me as War Leader. I'm on thin ice with them as it is.'

'The simplest solution would be not to go. Just leave the oracle alone.'

Lisutaris shakes her head. 'That won't satisfy my senior sorcerers. We've never gone to war without consulting the Goddess Vitina, and making the appropriate offerings. It's an important part of our beliefs, albeit a secret one. At least it was secret before you started rummaging through my private correspondence.'

'Do you actually believe in this oracle?' asks Makri, who's sceptical about anything supernatural.

'It's proved very accurate in the past. And helpful too. I intend to consult it. I need to do that without anyone knowing. That's why I'm taking you into my confidence. Thraxas, I need you to help me slip away unnoticed, and if anyone does notice, I need a good cover story. That seems like something you could manage.'

'Certainly. If you're set on it, it shouldn't be too difficult. How far off our route is it?'

'About half a day's ride. I'm planning on going with Ibella Hailstorm. She's the head of the Abelasian Sorcerers Guild. They're a small group but she's powerful, and a specialist in the old religion. Coranius the Grinder will accompany us.'

'How is Coranius?'

'As anti-social as ever. He's billeted on the far side of town, as far away from everyone as he can get. It's still good to have him around.'

'I hear he arrived with Tirini Snake Smiter.'

Lisutaris looks troubled at the mention of Tirini's name. 'She's in a bad way. The spell she used to get people out of Turai was too dangerous. She shouldn't have done it.'

'It saved Gurd's life.'

'I know. But it's almost wrecked Tirini's. She can hardly function. You can't travel instantly through the magic space without some bad effects. I'm worried about her but I don't have time to devote to her. I've asked one of the medical sorcerers, Saabril Eclipse, to look after her till she recovers.'

Lisutaris extinguishes her thazis stick. 'Time to get back to work. Captain Thraxas, have you made any progress?'

'None, Commander,' I admit. 'But I will.'

'I'm assigning two new recruits to your staff. Anumaris will introduce you. Make sure you're ready to leave tomorrow.'

The meeting ends. I return to my office upstairs. In an ideal world I'd get back on the couch and go to sleep, but my world hasn't been ideal for about thirty years and there's no reason for it to start now. Almost immediately Anumaris ushers two people inside.

'Our new members of staff.'

Chapter Six

I regard my new members of staff with suspicion. One young male sorcerer, not tall, quite dark-skinned, from somewhere south I'd say. The rainbow motif of the Sorcerers Guild is embroidered on his cloak in a curious fashion I've seen before but can't remember where. The other is a pale young Elf, even younger, with spiky yellow hair, a dull green tunic, and small bow slung across her back.

'This is–' begins Anumaris.

'I know who this is. Sendroo-ir-Vallis, from Avula. Commonly known as Droo. One of the most intoxicated young Elves ever seen in these or any parts.' I glare at her. 'You've been assigned to my security staff?'

The young Elf beams at me. 'My commander recommended me for special work!'

'Probably to get rid of you. You do appreciate we're engaged in dangerous war business here? Apart from drinking wine, writing poetry and falling out of trees, do you have any other qualifications?'

'Sendroo has an excellent record in her Elvish unit,' says Anumaris, briskly. For a young sorcerer, she does conduct herself with an air of confidence and efficiency. I'm not sure I like it.

'I believe Lisutaris placed her here because you know her already, and it's good to have a contact with the Elves.'

That may be, but Droo isn't the contact I'd have chosen. She's around eighteen, and from what I remember of my visit to the Isle of Avula, she was a friendly enough Elf, but I never saw any sign of an aptitude for security work. If the wartime situation wasn't so serious, I'd think that Lisutaris was mocking me.

'What rank are you?'

'Junior Ensign, Elvish Reconnaissance Regiment, temporarily seconded to the Sorcerers Auxiliary Regiment.' Droo is still beaming. Anumaris moves things along. 'This is Rinderan, from the Sorcerers Guild of the Southern Hills. He's a Senior Ensign in the Sorcerers Regiment.'

Now I remember where I've seen the curiously embroidered motif before. Princess Direeva wore the same device when she visited Turai during the great Sorcerers Assemblage at which Lisutaris was elected Head of the Guild. I'm interested to learn that Direeva - now Queen, and ruler of the Southern Hills - has sent us a sorcerer. Direeva is an ally of the west but she's in a very exposed position. Her realm lies in the southern part of the wastelands and faces continual threat from hostile Orcish nations. Direeva and her guild are renowned for the power of their sorcery. It's kept them safe till now, but I doubt she'd be able to withstand the full force of an attack from Prince Amrag's army.

'What's the situation in the Southern Hills?'

'Orcish forces are nearby but have not yet attacked. Queen Direeva will not give in to them, or allow them free access to the coast.'

That's good to hear, for the moment anyway. Were the Southern Hills to fall, the Orcish navy would have access to a lot of good anchorage. I study Rinderan. I often find it irritating meeting new sorcerers. They tend to remind me of my own past failures in the magic arts. Still, if he's been sent by Queen Direeva he's probably got a reasonable amount of power. That will be useful if we're to find Deeziz.

'Have you ever been in combat?'

'No,' he admits. 'I was too young for the last war.'

Young and inexperienced. My so-called staff have probably never seen a war dragon or a hostile Orc. If my regiment ends up advancing towards the enemy, I hope I've got some more experienced warriors by my side. I may be one of the most renowned fighters ever to buckle on a sword and march east, but I can't do it all myself. I take a seat at my desk. With my three members of staff in front of me, I'm briefly reminded of my days as a Senior Investigator at the Imperial Palace in Turai. That seems like a very long time ago.

'Commander Lisutaris believes that Deeziz the Unseen is on her way here to spy on us. We can't allow that to happen. If she manages to infiltrate our senior command there's no telling what harm she'll do. At the very least, she'll pass information about our plans to the enemy. At worst, she might assassinate our commanders, or sabotage supply lines. We have to find her and stop her.'

'Surely no Orcish sorcerer could arrive in secret?' says Rinderan. 'Our own sorcerers would detect her.'

'She's already proved she can do it. She came into Turai and no one spotted her. Completely fooled the Turanian security services, which admittedly wasn't all that difficult. But she fooled Lisutaris too, which is difficult. She fooled me too, which is next to impossible. We've underestimated the Orcish Sorcerers Guild for a long time.'

'Then how can we find her? She could be anywhere.'

'Good point.' I reach out for a beer. I realise there's no beer on my desk. I look at Anumaris. 'What happened to my beer?'

'What beer?'

'The beer you should have brought me as part of your duties.'

'That's not part of my duties. Lisutaris told me–'

'I'm your commanding officer. I say what your duties are. Where was I?'

'The Orcish Sorcerers Guild.'

'Right. They're powerful. Foul Orcs, but powerful. Furthermore, their army is a lot better organised these days. I saw their phalanxes outside Turai. If we're going to defeat them we need everyone to pull their weight. Not, for instance, refuse to carry out orders from their commanding officer when he requests a ready supply of beer.'

My three members of staff are looking confused. I realise I might have strayed off course a little. 'The point is, we need to be well-organised in our search. Deeziz might be anywhere but I think she'll try and infiltrate our ranks at the highest level possible. That means everyone at headquarters is a suspect.'

'Everyone?'

'Yes. Apart from me. And Lisutaris and Makri. I've been with them constantly since Turai fell. I know they're actually who they say they are. For everyone else, I want a background check. The guards on duty, the junior ranks, the senior ranks, everyone. Everyone who's close to Lisutaris needs to be checked out. Make

34

sure they didn't suffer any mysterious disappearance on the way here, or have any time they can't account for. Any one of these people could actually be Deeziz.'

'The people we're meant to check on - does it include the commanders? General Hemistos? Bishop-General Ritari?'

'Yes. Droo, you're to question them about their movements in the past month. Anumaris and Rinderan, you use your sorcery to probe for anything suspicious.'

'They're not going to like that,' says Anumaris.

'Probably not. Be discreet if you can. But if you can't be discreet, don't worry about it. I'm in charge of Lisutaris's personal security so I have the authority. Any complaints, refer them to me. Or I should say, try and get rid of them first. But if you can't get rid of them, refer them to me.'

Junior Ensign Droo grins, and salutes, enthusiastically. Rinderan and Anumaris, rather less so.

'Meanwhile I'll be conducting searches around town, looking to pick up information in places of interest before we leave. Any further questions?'

There being no further questions, I send my staff out to begin their work. I place a minor locking spell on my door, and settle down on the couch to complete my unfinished nap. I'm satisfied with my day's work. It doesn't take long for me to get things moving. Thraxas, number one chariot at investigating. I'm just drifting off when there's a heavy knock on my door. I attempt to ignore it. It comes again, louder.

'Thraxas, I know you're in there.'

I curse. It's Makri. I know from experience there's no point in trying to ignore her. She'd only break the door down. I drag myself off the couch and haul the door open.

'Is this important? I was engaged in some serious work.'

'You were sleeping on the couch.' Makri strides into the room, smiling broadly. She doesn't smile broadly all that often.

'What are you looking so happy about?'

'Gurd and Tanrose. I didn't think we'd see them again. I missed them.'

'I missed them too. I thought old Gurd might have finally handed in his toga, without me there to protect him.'

'And we're ready to march! We're going to kick these Orcs out of Turai!'

Makri grew up as an Orcish gladiator, in effect a slave. She hates them bitterly. 'Do you think the Orcs will come out and fight? Or will they hide in Turai?'

'I don't know. Whatever they do, they'll make life difficult for us. Prince Amrag's a good commander.'

Makri looks at me quizzically. 'Did you just compliment an Orc?'

'Maybe. There's no point pretending he's not a good commander. He's given us the runaround so far. Are you going to tell Lisutaris that you're related to him?'

'No.'

Makri is Amrag's sister, or half-sister. She has a complicated ancestry which she's never fully explained. Amrag is older than her, and lacks her Elvish blood, but they're related. No one knows that except me. I've told her she should inform Lisutaris but she refuses. Understandable, I suppose. She's had a tough enough time without giving people an excuse to be even more suspicious of her.

'Makri, do you have to keep grinning like that? It's unnatural.'

'I thought you'd be happy too. You're always going on about what a great soldier you were. Aren't you looking forward to some fighting?'

'I might be, if I wasn't stuck in the Sorcerers Auxiliary Regiment with a bunch of callow incompetents.'

'Callow incompetents?'

'You know Lisutaris assigned Droo to my unit? What am I meant to do with an eighteen-year-old Elf who's only life experience is sitting in trees writing poetry? As for Anumaris Thunderbolt, she has some sort of mania against alcohol. Hardly a minute passes but she's lecturing me about not drinking so much. I suspect Lisutaris has deliberately assigned me the most unsuitable staff out of spite.'

Makri laughs. 'Or perhaps she just doesn't want you rolling around drunk when you're meant to be investigating. You should follow her example. She's really cut down on her thazis intake since she was made War Leader.'

'So she claims. She's probably still sucking it up in private. Anyway, you wouldn't catch me and Gurd going into battle without a few ales inside us. Ale is the bedrock of a good phalanx. Not that there's any chance of me being in a good phalanx while I'm shepherding these untrained youths around the place. She's sent me this sorcerer called Rinderan from the Southern Hills and he's never even been in combat. Probably flee at the first sign of a dragon.'

'We've all got to make sacrifices. We're engaged in important business.'

I glower at Makri. 'Since when did you become the voice of wisdom?'

'Since I became Ensign Makri in the Sorcerers Auxiliary Regiment, bodyguard to our War Leader, Commander Lisutaris, Mistress of the Sky. I've put aside all frivolities for the duration of the war. Nothing will affect my concentration on the job in hand and I advise you to adopt the same attitude.'

Makri draws herself up, looks serious, and opens the door. 'I'll see you on the march, Captain Thraxas.'

Makri can be hard to take at the best of times. This new, responsible version is worse than most. She departs. I head for the couch. Before I can reach it the door bursts open and Makri flies into the room.

'Hide me!' she cries, before slamming the door shut and diving behind the makeshift couch.

Rather puzzled, I look down at her crouching figure. 'What's the matter?'

'See-ath!'

'What?'

'See-ath! The Elf from Avula. he's outside in the corridor. I can't let him see me.'

'Is See-ath the one–'

'Yes!' hisses Makri.

Poor Makri. She's strongly attracted to Elves. Elves, unfortunately, tend to be suspicious of her because of her Orcish blood. That's not to say they don't find her attractive. Most people find Makri attractive, particularly in the chainmail bikini she wore as a barmaid. But when she did finally get her chance, and embarked on a brief fling with a young Elf on the Isle of Avula, it didn't end well. So I understand, anyway. She's never volunteered many details of the affair.

I look at her with interest. 'What happened to "I've put aside all frivolities for the duration of the war?"'

'That was before I knew See-ath was here.'

'You can't spend the whole war hiding behind my couch.'

'Why not?'

'We have to march north tomorrow, for one thing. Is it really so bad seeing him again?'

'Yes.'

'Come on Makri, people have unfortunate relationships all the time. So it didn't work out. That's not so bad. Maybe a little embarrassing, nothing more.'

'It's a lot more.'

'Why? What happened on Avula?'

Makri, still hiding behind the couch, screws up her face. 'Avula wasn't so bad. It was afterwards.'

'Afterwards? But you didn't see him afterwards.'

'I know. I was upset that he didn't get in touch. I sent him some messages.'

'Messages? How?'

'By ship. And by sorcerer. Once by carrier pigeon.'

'I see. What did these messages say?'

'They started off saying I missed him and why hadn't he got in touch? Then I got a little upset, and I... well...'

'You threatened him with violence?'

'By the ninth message I told him I was going to chop his head off and feed it to a dragon. Maybe that was the tenth, I forget exactly.'

'I can see why things have become awkward. That's not really normal behaviour.'

'I'm not very experienced at these things.'

I shake my head. Poor Makri.

'What'll I do?' she wails.

'How about facing him manfully, or womanfully, if there is such a word, and discussing it?'

'Out of the question. I can never see him again.'

'Then what's your plan?'

'Didn't you once mention some place in the furthest west? I could flee there.'

'For goodness sake Makri.' I drag her out from behind the couch. 'You can't hide forever. You might not even see him again. He's young, isn't he? That means he's not a senior figure in the Elvish military. He probably just arrived at headquarters to deliver a message or something like that. Once the armies march tomorrow you'll have thousands of men between you and him.'

Makri considers this. 'You might be right. Could you check the corridor for me?'

I open the door and stick my head out. There's no one there, Elvish or otherwise. 'The coast is clear. Do you need me to walk you back to Lisutaris?'

Makri peers out into the corridor. 'I'm all right. But don't lock your door in case I need to run back here.'

With that, Makri, champion gladiator of the Orcish lands, undefeated in combat since she arrived in the west, winner of the great sword-fighting competition in Samsarina, and now personal bodyguard to the Commander of the Western Army, creeps furtively out into the corridor like a guilty schoolgirl returning late from her holidays. It's a pathetic sight. I shake my head sadly, and finally mange to return to my couch for my long-delayed afternoon sleep.

Chapter Seven

Despite their inexperience, my security unit proves to be adept at the tasks I've given them. The previously intoxicated and irresponsible Droo almost seems like a reformed character. She hurries around, gathering information, writing things down, and generally doing everything that's asked of her. She appears to be enjoying herself. It's the first time she's left the Elvish islands, so I suppose it's all quite exciting for her. As for Anumaris and Rinderan, the young sorcerers manage to be both tactful and efficient while carrying out their security checks. I wouldn't have been surprised to find myself confronted by angry senior officers, furious at the suggestion that their backgrounds needed looking in to, but so far it hasn't happened. Anumaris and Rinderan mange to establish a coherent and uninterrupted timeline for both Bishop-General Ritari and General Hemistos. Neither of them have gone missing recently, or suffered any unexpected interruptions to their normal routines. For the past few months neither of them have been alone for any length of time. That, along with some sorcerous investigation, seems to rule out the possibility of either of them being an impostor. I'm keenly aware of Deeziz's power, but I'm now reasonably certain that neither our infantry commander nor our cavalry commander are fakes. As they're the closest people to Lisutaris, that's a relief. I instruct Anumaris and Rinderan to look into the background of their immediate subordinates.

'Pay special attention to Bishop-General Ritari's second-in-command, Legate Apiroi. I'm suspicious of him.'

'Why?'

'Because he's been complaining about Lisutaris filling her staff with low-class Turanians. Sounds like a trouble-maker to me. Could be an Orcish spy.'

We're still checking up on Lord Kalith-ar-Yil, something Droo takes to with great enthusiasm. She finds it funny that's she's investigating an Elf Lord, who, back in his own realm, would be immune from any sort of enquiry.

Anumaris and Rinderan share some similarities in character, and even in appearance. They're both young sorcerers with good reputations, they both have long dark hair and always wear their sorcerers' cloaks. Each is rather methodical, not a bad trait in the circumstances. Neither are what you'd call gregarious, but Rinderan does hold one big advantage over Anumaris. The sorcerer from the Southern Hills is an unexpected authority on beer. His family own a brewery. I'm impressed.

'A whole brewery? They own it?'

'It's the largest of its kind in the Southern Hills. We supply all the taverns in the region. I was meant to go into the family business until I turned out to have a talent for sorcery. I went to sorcerers college instead. My father was disappointed but my mother was proud. We've never had a sorcerer in the family before.'

'What do you brew?'

'Dark ale mainly, but we make a good mild ale too. We use hops and barley from our own farms.'

'I've never heard anything more interesting from a sorcerer. Tell me more.'

At this moment we're loading equipment onto our wagon. I'd expected to be marching, but as an integral part of Lisutaris's command, we've been given a covered wagon. We'll be riding along not far behind our War Leader. I dump my armour in the back, though I take more care with my sword, a new Elvish blade given to me by Makri. It was part of her prize for winning the great sword-fighting tournament. It was a good prize, and a fine gift. So good that I didn't know how to thank her properly, leading to an awkward silence, as I recall. Rinderan is just describing the brewing process when Anumaris bustles up and interrupts us with some footling enquiry about provisions. I attempt to brush her off but Anumaris is persistent, and difficult to brush off.

'We're leaving in three hours,' she insists. 'I need to make sure this check-list of provisions is complete.'

I glance at the list. 'You forgot the beer.'

'We're not bringing any beer.'

I'm really starting to dislike her. I send Droo off to find beer and get back to my conversation with Rinderan. The scene all around is chaotic as the army prepares to march. Orders are being shouted

41

from all directions. Trumpets sound as officers struggle to get their men in order. Huge dust clouds billow from the north where the cavalry are manoeuvring into position. Getting an army moving is no easy task. The fact that we're still on schedule is further testament to Lisutaris's powers of organisation.

I haven't had much further opportunity of talking with Gurd, though I did meet him briefly. Gurd had joined up with the Turanian phalanx, but to his dismay, he was immediately seconded to the Sorcerers Auxiliary Regiment, the same as me. He's not particularly happy about it. He wanted to be in the front lines, and worries that he won't see any fighting.

'Protecting sorcerers? That's no task for a warrior.'

Gurd is older than me, and I'm in my mid-forties. You might say that a position in a leading phalanx is no task for a man that age either. You wouldn't actually say that out loud to Gurd, obviously, or he'd knock you unconscious, but it might be the reason for his secondment. Or he might be there by request of whichever Turanian officer was responsible for assigning duties. Gurd is known in the city as a man you can trust. If he turned out to be the only person between a vulnerable sorcerer and a horde of Orcs, he's not going to flee. I'm still heartened by his re-appearance, and wonder if any of my other old friends escaped from the city. Captain Rallee, for instance. *Old friend* might not be quite the right term for Rallee. We seemed to find ourselves on opposing sides more often than not, him being a civil guard and me being a private investigator, Even so, I've known him a long time, and I hope he survived. I'm loading my last bag of supplies into the wagon when Droo trots into view with a crate of beer cradled in her arms and a grin on her face.

'I've got the beer, enormous human.'

'Captain Thraxas would be the correct form of address.'

'Also, Lord Kalith-ar-Yil wants to see you.'

'What for?'

'Something about "Young elves who ought to be thrown in prison for insubordination and wait till he gets his hands on that damned rogue Thraxas who probably put her up to it."'

'I take it he didn't appreciate your security checks?'

42

'Not much. He objected quite violently when I asked him what he had for breakfast for the past thirty days. You know he was missing from the island for a day? He claims it was his standard religious duty as Lord of Avula but it could be suspicious.' Young Sendroo looks quite happy at the thought. She's enjoying the opportunity of disconcerting her Elf Lord. I warm to her insubordinate spirit.

'Good work,' I tell her. 'Keep it up. I want you to check every Elf who's anywhere near Lisutaris. Any complaints, inform them that Captain Thraxas, Chief Security Officer of the Commander's Personal Security Unit, has given you full authorisation to make their lives uncomfortable.'

Droo departs to collect her belongings.

'You don't really think Lord Kalith-ar-Yil could be Deeziz the Unseen, do you?' asks Anumaris.

'Not really. But he gave me a hard time when I was on his island. I don't mind seeing him discomfited.'

'Do we even know that Deeziz can impersonate a man? Or a male Elf?'

'No, we don't. In Turai she appeared as a female singer. But before that we thought she was male. There doesn't seem to be any firm evidence either way. Given her powers, it's best to assume she could impersonate anyone.'

When our wagon is fully loaded with provisions, arms and sundry equipment, we have a very long wait as the units of the army still within the walls of the city trundle slowly through the great gates to join those assembled outside. Rinderan takes the reigns with Anumaris beside him while Droo and I sit in the back. We're just on the point of passing through the gate when Makri unexpectedly clambers into the wagon and lies on the floor. I look down at her. Despite her fervour for war, she hasn't cut her hair, which is extremely long and thick, and now covers quite a large part of the wagon's wooden, slatted flooring.

'Shouldn't you be guarding our War Leader?'

'Top secret conference,' she explains. 'Only Lisutaris, Hemistos, Ritari and Kalith allowed. I've been excused. I thought I'd see how you were.'

'I see.'

We move slowly through the gate into the fields outside.

'Is that the only reason you're here?'

'Why do you ask?'

'Because you're lying on the floor looking like a woman who's hiding from someone.'

'Why is Makri hiding?' ask Droo.

'Because she has the emotional maturity of a five-year-old and can't face her Elvish ex-lover.'

Makri looks anguished. 'They've made him a Liaison Officer! Why did they do that? He's always bringing messages to Lisutaris. I have to keep ducking out of sight.'

'Makri, this is pitiful. You can't spend the entire war hiding from an Elf. We're meant to be on the same side.'

'Maybe I'll get lucky,' says Makri. 'I might get killed quickly.'

Throughout this, young Droo has been listening. 'What's this about? What happened?'

'Makri had a brief affair when we visited your island. Apparently it didn't finish well. He never contacted her afterwards.'

'Ooh!' Droo is very interested in this. 'Who was it? Maybe I know him.'

'His name was See-ath,' mumbles Makri, still taking care to keep herself out of sight.

Droo laughs, rather tactlessly. 'See-ath? That explains it.'

'What do you mean?'

'See-ath has hundreds of lovers. He's famous for it.'

'No he isn't,' says Makri, angrily. 'He told me he was shy and hardly talks to women.'

At this, Droo positively explodes with mirth. Makri flushes an angry shade of red.

'Stop laughing!'

'Sorry. But it's funny. Really, See-ath isn't shy with women. He's had lots of lovers.'

'How many?'

'Probably one a week. No, that's an exaggeration. One a month. No, that's not quite right either. Say one every two weeks or so. Two a month. Maybe little more.'

Makri's face is grim. 'He told me I was special.'

'You sent him a sorcerous message threatening to cut his head off.' I point out. 'That probably counts as special. Not in a good way, obviously.'

'Oh God.' Makri buries her face in her hands. 'I can't believe I sent him all these messages. I'll have to flee. Tell Lisutaris I caught the plague and you had to bury me quickly.'

At that moment Lisutaris hauls herself into the wagon, quite athletically. 'Why is Makri pretending to die of the plague? I thought you were keen to go to war? Makri, I expected better of you.'

'It's private,' says Makri, hopelessly.

'Not that private,' says Droo. 'Thraxas knows about it. So do I. See-ath probably told a few people as well, especially if you've been threatening to chop his head off.'

Makri cringes. I struggle not to laugh. There's something engaging about Droo's lack of tact.

'What's this?' demands Lisutaris. She looks pointedly at Makri. Makri unwillingly explains her situation again. Lisutaris seems interested, then frowns. 'Last year I remember asking the communications sorcerer Jurias if he could send an important message to the Elvish Isles. He said it would have to wait, as he'd used up all his magic for another client. He needed time to recover. Was that your doing?'

'It might have been,' says Makri, gloomily. 'I did send a lot of messages.'

'Fascinating,' I say. 'Who'd have thought that Makri's hopeless romance would end up destroying the war effort?'

'Could we stop talking about this?' demands Makri. 'I'm over it now anyway.' She rises to her feet, looking quite fierce.

'I'd no idea you had a history with See-ath,' says Lisutaris. 'It does sound embarrassing. But perhaps he won't remember you?'

'Not much chance of that,' I say. 'Makri was the only person with Orcish blood ever to land on Avula. She made quite an impression. After she fell in their ceremonial pool they had to perform a special ritual to cleanse it.'

'Could we talk about something else?' says Makri. She scowls. 'I've had enough of Elves.'

Lisutaris brings the conversation to an end by telling Ensign Droo that she's here to discuss a private matter with her Chief Security Officer, meaning me.

'I'll see if I can find more beer,' says Droo cheerfully, as she hops out of the wagon.

'I see she's fitting in well with your unit,' says Lisutaris, as the young Elf departs. 'I'm here to talk about our visit to the oracle. We'll be leaving tomorrow night. Be ready to meet outside the camp after midnight.'

'Commander, I'm still worried about this excursion. If Deeziz the Unseen has infiltrated our forces already then she might know about it. It would be the perfect opportunity for an ambush. I don't think you should go.'

'I won't be defenceless. Coranius, Ibella and I can muster a lot of sorcerous power. You'll be with me. And Makri.'

'I don't like it either.' Makri shakes her head. 'All it would take would be one well placed arrow when you were vulnerable.'

'It's very risky, leaving the army and trailing off through the countryside in a small group. You're our War Leader. The west needs you.'

Lisutaris doesn't dismiss our concerns out of hand, but she won't be swayed. 'There might be some risk, but it's small. No one apart from your unit and Hanama knows we're going.'

'I haven't finished security checks on Hanama yet.'

'I assure you she really is Hanama.'

I'm unmoved. 'I'll be checking her anyway.'

Lisutaris doesn't object to me being thorough. 'General Hemistos and Bishop-General Ritari have already complained about your staff bothering them with their security checks. I told them they had to put up with it. The same for Lord Kalith. Nonetheless, it really is Hanama.'

'She might be an impostor.'

'I know her much better than you realise, Thraxas.'

'How? Through the Association of Gentlewomen?'

'The membership of that organisation is unknown,' says Lisutaris, and moves the conversation on briskly. 'The journey to the Oracle will take seven hours. We'll be back in a day. I have to do it. If I didn't consult the Oracle before going to war, it would damage morale in the Sorcerers Guild. As long as we keep it secret from Bishop-General Ritari and the rest of the religious fanatics, it will be fine.'

Lisutaris sounds confident. For a woman who's under a lot of pressure, she's bearing up well. General opinion among the army so far is that she's a good choice as War Leader.

'Have the Abelasian sorcerers made any progress with their spells for identifying Deeziz?'

Lisutaris shakes her head. 'No. We've been gathering up everything we know about her. I even had Ibella Hailstorm delve into my own memories to see if there was anything I'd forgotten from our encounter in the Avenging Axe, and normally I'd rather not have anyone delving around in my memories, even a friend like Ibella. So far it hasn't given us anything. They haven't developed a spell to locate her. They'll keep trying.'

'Are we going to wait on the border for the Orcs or march right back to Turai?'

'Were you trying to take me by surprise with that question?'

'Yes.'

'Then I'm surprised,' says Lisutaris. 'But I can't tell you. That's a secret matter for my command council.'

'Have you made a decision?'

'I can't tell you that either.' Our War Leader turns to her bodyguard. 'Are you ready to resume your duties, Ensign Makri?'

Makri nods. 'I apologise for the temporary lapse. I won't let See-ath bother me again.'

'Good. We can't let minor personal problems interfere with our work. I could have found Kublinos a distraction, but I brushed his attentions off without a second thought.'

That's something of an exaggeration. Kublinos the Samsarinan Harbour Sorcerer took a great shine to Lisutaris and I wouldn't say she brushed his attentions off easily. I remember her hiding in a tavern, unable to cope with his wooing. Lisutaris and Makri depart. There's a shouted command from one of the marshals responsible for getting the army moving, and our wagon rumbles forward. Droo hops aboard with a bottle of wine in her hand.

'Look what I found!'

She passes me the bottle. I drink deeply. I like Droo. She's a good addition to the unit.

Chapter Eight

After two days of travelling, the rich farmlands of Samsarina still stretch out endlessly in front of us.

'You know what I hate about Samsarina?'

'What?' says Droo.

'There's too much farmland.'

The young Elf laughs. 'I don't dislike it. But I'm used to more trees.'

It's not only the farmland that stretches out ahead. We're following a long column of troops, steadily making their way north-east. Their passing raises a huge cloud of dust which drifts over the array of wagons bringing up the rear. Sitting with the reins in my hand, I have a light scarf tied over my face to keep the dust from my lungs, as does Droo, and most of the people towards the rear of the column. So far, we've advanced without incident. Ahead of the column, and flanking us in the distance, Lisutaris has sorcerers on patrol, protected by units from the Sorcerers Auxiliary Regiment. They're there to give us advance warning of any trouble. We're not expecting to meet Orcish forces just yet but we can't be too careful. Prince Amrag already surprised us by bringing dragons in winter to Turai, something that had never been done before. Samsarina should be out of range of his dragons, but his powerful sorcerers guild might have been working on ways of allowing them to travel further.

Rinderan and Anumaris are in the back of the wagon. When the army stops marching, or one of its regular meal breaks, all four of us will resume our task of hunting for anything suspicious among our forces. If it sounds like a tenuous enterprise, it is. I haven't come up with anything particularly brilliant. There again, neither have the sorcerers tasked with the same thing. Irith Victorious hasn't invented any sort of spell that might help. So Lisutaris informs me, anyway. I haven't seen Irith yet. I should, but I'm still wary of the encounter. It's going to be uncomfortable.

'What if Deeziz isn't even here?' wonders Droo. 'Maybe she decided to stay with the Orcs this time.'

'Possible. But Lisutaris thought she caught a glimpse of her making her way west. Lisutaris is good at that sort of thing. I'd say there's a strong chance Deeziz is somewhere in the midst of this army right now.'

'What do you think she's planning? Sabotage?'

'Maybe. Though I can't see the most powerful Orcish sorcerer wasting her time on petty acts of destruction. I suppose she could try working some devastating spell, but that would be difficult with so many human sorcerers around. Even if they don't know what's coming they've always got their dampening field in place. Makes it hard for any spell to take us unawares. Sorcerers do a lot of dampening. When it comes to battle, they're a lot less exciting than you'd expect.'

'How do you mean?'

'Each side tends to cancel out the other. They use a lot of power defending their own armies by preventing their opponent's spells from landing. Or preventing them being launched in the first place. It can end up as a war of attrition, with no one getting an advantage.'

'So what happens then?'

'It's left to the regular soldiers to hack each other to pieces. Last time there was a major invasion our sorcerers managed to hold off their guild, but they had enough troops to make it all the way to the walls of Turai. They had dragons, which gives them an advantage. Turai would have fallen if the Elves hadn't arrived.'

'Why didn't we save you this time?'

'Because the Orcs attacked in winter. Damned uncivilised behaviour, when you think about it. War is mean to be a summer pursuit.'

'Well, we're here now,' says Droo, and looks happy about it.

Droo is a cheerful young Elf. Sitting in this wagon, breathing in the dust of a huge army, is far removed from the life she's used to, but she hasn't complained about anything. It's a point in her favour. Since I last encountered her, she seems to have become a lot more responsible. Perhaps I was a good influence. A trumpet sounds in the distance. It's taken up by others. Time to eat, and rest. It's just past midday and we'll be halted for an hour or so. Rinderan and

Anumaris both poke their heads through the canvas that separates the back of the wagon from the driver's seat.

'Any new instructions?' asks Anumaris.

'Same as always. Look for anything strange.'

Rinderan frowns. 'Anything strange is so vague. We're in the midst of a huge marching army. It's hard to know what's strange and what isn't.'

'Just keep your eyes and ears open. If you come across something really strange, you'll recognise it.'

'How?'

'I don't know. Deeziz hasn't sent us instructions on how to find her. Just wander around, talk to people and see what you can learn.'

They depart together, Rinderan still unsatisfied. I clamber down from the pillion.

'Where are we going?' asks Droo.

'Wherever we can get a drink. Gurd and his cohort aren't far away. If we're lucky, Tanrose will be cooking.'

'Will we get any investigating done there?'

'As much as anywhere else. Let Rinderan and Anumaris wander around asking questions, they enjoy it.'

We walk through a mass of soldiers. A few are spending their break sleeping, while others busy themselves making a quick meal, something at which seasoned campaigners are well-practiced. Tanrose has never been on a military campaign before, as far as I know, but she's such a talented cook she can produce excellent meals in any circumstances.

'Tanrose likes her food to be appreciated,' I tell Droo. 'That's why I eat so much of it. It helps her.'

Gurd and a few other Turanian exiles are gathered round a small fire. Above the fire is a metal tripod, from which hangs a pot, the contents of which are simmering gently. Tanrose stands over it, adding spices.

'Back already?' Gurd laughs. 'Don't they feed you in the security unit?'

'Not as well as Tanrose feeds you. I've brought you a flagon of wine so stop hogging that stew and let a proper eater in for his share.'

Gurd hasn't quite got over his chagrin at being placed in the Sorcerers Auxiliary Regiment. He's none too pleased to find himself in one of the squadrons designated as protection for Lisutaris, and still hopes he'll see more action. 'It's not going to be much of a war if we're stuck at the back all the time, protecting sorcerers.'

'We'll see plenty of action. Lisutaris will end up in the thick of things. '

'How can you be sure?'

'Because we're not strong enough to beat the Orcs without her sorcery.'

Tanrose is concerned. 'I don't like the thought of you coming so close to the Orcish sorcerers.'

'Don't worry. When these sorcerers are concentrating on their spells they're quite susceptible to a swift thrust from a spear. Seen it happen plenty of times. We'll be fine. As long as I'm good shape. You know, plenty of pies and that sort of thing.'

'I'm sorry Thraxas, I can't make a pie on this little campfire. I'd need some sort of oven.'

I don't try to hide my disappointment. 'I'm fading away. By the time we meet the Orcs I'll be a shadow of myself.'

'I don't think there's much chance of that,' says Tanrose, eyeing my waistline.

I settle down to eat a bowl of Tanrose's stew. Talk of pies and ovens reminds me of a man called Erisox. Back in Turai, he made good batch in his portable oven while there were dragons attacking overhead. He did tell me a lot of lies when I was investigating him, but I forgave him because of his pies. Thinking of that case reminds of Turai's highest official, Consul Kalius.

'Has there been any news of the Consul? Or the Royal family?'

None of the Turanians around Gurd's campfire have heard anything. The general opinion is that our ageing, ailing King and his family probably perished, along with their senior officials. The palace and main institutions of government were all close to the northern walls where the Orcs broke through. By that time, Deputy Consul Cicerius was in effective control of the city. Cicerius was a better man that the Consul, but there's been no news of him either. At this moment Turai has no government. What will happen if we retake the city, no one knows.

For a few moments there's a peaceable atmosphere as everyone enjoys Tanrose's cooking. It doesn't last.

'Where is this vagabond Captain Thraxas? Take me to him!'

Whoever's angry with Captain Thraxas has a strong Niojan accent. I look up to see Legate Apiroi storming towards me with Anumaris and Rinderan trailing in his wake. The Legate, second-in-command to Bishop-General Ritari, is a large man with closely-cropped hair and a permanent scowl. He wears the austere black tunic of the Niojan officer class and carries a short sword in a scabbard at his waist.

'Captain Thraxas!' he roars. 'Are you responsible for this outrage?'

I clamber to my feet. 'Probably. What outrage are we talking about?'

'The outrage of your lackeys daring to doubt me! It was bad enough when they demanded details of my past movements. An impertinent request to which I'd have given short shrift had not our War Leader urged us to comply. And now I find they've been checking up on the answers I gave them! How dare you order them to do that! If a Niojan Officer deigns to answer your foolish security questions, you will take him at his word, not sneak around behind his back!'

Behind him, Anumaris and Rinderan are looking flustered, obviously unsure how to react to the wrath of this senior officer.

'Well, you Turanian dog!' continues the Legate. 'What do you have to say for yourself?'

I turn to Anumaris Thunderbolt. 'Have you finished your background checks on Legate Apiroi?'

'Not quite, Captain.'

'Then carry on with them till you have.'

'What?' The Legate practically explodes with rage. 'You dare to insult me, second-in-command to Bishop-General Ritari? I'll have your head for this!'

I look him in the eye. 'Everyone close to Commander Lisutaris needs to be checked out. No exceptions. Orders from the War Leader herself. If you don't like it, tough. Maybe you've got something to hide?'

Beside me, Gurd has risen to his feet, ready to come to my aid if the Legate draws his sword and attacks me, which doesn't seem that unlikely. Apiroi steps forward so his face is almost touching mine.

'You'll pay for this insult. A Niojan Legate does not have to answer to a man like you. It's bad enough our War Leader employs a filthy Orc as a bodyguard without her filling her personal staff with low-born Turanians. I warn you Captain, if the Bishop-General or I are bothered by your Security Unit again, there will be dire consequences.'

Legate Apiroi glares at me, Anumaris and Rinderan. Having satisfied himself that he's done enough glaring, he storms off.

'Touchy fellow,' says Gurd.

'Niojans are never that friendly.'

'What should we do?' asks Rinderan.

'Sit down and have some stew and a cup of wine. Then get back to checking up on him. He's a suspicious character.'

'Is that really wise?' Rinderan looks nervous.

'Wise or not, we're doing it. No one escapes the attention of my security unit.'

'What if he attacks us?'

'You're sorcerers. You should be safe enough.'

'Senior Niojan officers have a lot of spell protection,' says Anumaris.

'Then poke him in the eye with a stick. Now are we going to stand here taking all day or are we going to eat?'

Tanrose's stew is one of the finest meals I've eaten since I left Turai. She has a way of seasoning and simmering that brings out the best in even the most basic of ingredients. After several large bowlfuls I'm feeling optimistic about our prospects.

'We'll chase these Orcs back where they came from.'

So beneficial is Tanrose's cooking to my state of mind that I don't even object when I'm approached by an unfamiliar sorcerer on my way back to my wagon.

'Captain Thraxas? I've been looking for you.'

'Why? And who are you?'

'Saabril Clearwater. Medical sorcerer, first class, from Kamara. Commander Lisutaris assigned me to look after Tirini Snake Smiter.'

'I see.'

Saabril Clearwater is around thirty, fair haired and fair skinned. She speaks with a rather unusual accent, though one I've heard before, from the few Kamaran mercenaries I've encountered on my travels. Kamara is a very small nation, a long way west, near Kastlin. Its citizens aren't often found this far east. I don't think I've ever met a Kamaran sorcerer before.

'How is Tirini?'

'Not very well. Lisutaris thought you might be able to help.'

I don't mind the thought of helping Tirini, after she helped Gurd and Tanrose escape from Turai, but I've no idea how. If a Medical Sorcerer, First Class, isn't able to heal her, I'm certainly not going to be able to. Saabril asks me if I'd accompany her to see Tirini, who's resting up in a small wagon of her own, not far from Lisutaris's travelling command centre. All around, soldiers and camp followers are finishing off their meals, packing up, and making ready to move.

'What's wrong with Tirini?'

'It's difficult to say. Making an instant journey through the magic space is very dangerous. You can collide with anything. A sharp object might go through your body or take your head off. Then there are the strange energy fields. Sorcerers think these are responsible for the way the space shifts continually, but we don't really understand them. Travelling through an energy field just as it changes might have a terrible effect. But really, I don't know what's wrong with Tirini. Her body seems healthy enough but she's not recovering the way she should.'

By this time we've reached the small wagon. I climb in after Saabril. I'm not prepared for the sight that greets me. Tirini, famed for her beauty, fashionable outfits and expensive accessories, looks rather like one of the poor women you might see begging around the docks in Turai. She's wrapped up in a decent enough blanket but her body seems shrunken. Her face is lined and her eyes are watery. Her hair, previously the brightest blond ever seen at a fashionable party at the Imperial Palace, is lank and dull. Dark roots are showing prominently around her scalp. She wears no jewellery and her feet are encased in a pair of old slippers which she'd rather have died than been seen wearing back in Turai. I'm shocked. She seems to have aged twenty years in the space of a few months. I'm not certain how to greet her. 'Hello Tirini,' I venture.

She doesn't respond. There's a bowl of soup lying next to her on a small table but it doesn't look like it's been touched. I look towards Saabril Clearwater.

'She doesn't speak much,' says the sorcerer, softly.

Distressing as this is, I'm still not clear as to why Saabril has asked me here. I have no medical skills, apart from the rough-and-ready sort a man learns on the battlefield, for patching up comrades till they can find proper attention. If Tirini crashed through some harmful energy field in the magic space, thereby frying her brain, there's nothing I can do about it. Maybe there's nothing anybody can do about it.

Tirini mumbles something inaudible.

'What was that?'

'They took my shoes,' she says, a little louder.

'Who took your shoes? What shoes?'

'They took my shoes.' Tirini sounds unbearably sad. Her voice tails off. She closes her eyes.

'What does she mean? Who took her shoes?'

'I don't know, but that's all she ever says. Commander Lisutaris thought you might be able to help. She told me you were an investigator.'

'It helps if I know what I'm investigating. Are we talking about an actual pair of shoes?'

56

'I don't know.'

'Are these shoes important for her health?'

'I don't know that either. But none of my treatments are working and she's getting worse.'

It crosses my mind to say something harsh to the Medical Sorcerer, pointing out that we're in the middle of a war and I've already got more than enough vital work to be getting on with. But I'm discomfited by the sight of Tirini Snake Smiter in such a poor state, so I remain silent. We leave the wagon.

'Is she suffering the effects of some hostile spell?' I ask.

'None that I can find. Nor Lisutaris. Neither of us can diagnose the problem, or do anything that seems to help.' Saabril looks at me quite apologetically. 'I know you're busy, but Lisutaris asked me to consult you, just in case you could discover anything.'

'I'll see what I can do.'

I turn and leave, heading back towards my own wagon. I'm unsettled by what I've just seen. More unsettled than I'd have imagined I would be. In Turai, Tirini was a vain woman who, as far as I could see, was a frivolous waste of time. She seemed to spend her entire life indulging in scandalous affairs while wasting her money on endless streams of fancy clothes and expensive trinkets. She probably spent more on her hair every week than the poor of Turai had to feed their families for a year. On the few occasions we met, she made it clear she regarded me as her inferior in every way.

I bump into Makri just outside my wagon, and tell her about my encounter with the ailing Tirini.

'Is that why you're looking gloomy?'

'I suppose so.'

'But you never liked her.'

'I know. She's a frivolous idiot. But she's our frivolous idiot. Having a glamorous sorcerer spending a ridiculous amount of money on golden fur cloaks and pink shoes, and outraging the Bishops by her disreputable behaviour, was part of what made Turai what it was.' I shake my head. 'I didn't like to see her the way she is now. Especially after she rescued Gurd and Tanrose.'

'What are you going to do?'

'I don't know. Find out what she meant by "they took my shoes," I suppose. It might mean something.'

Makri is dressed in her lightweight Orcish armour; dark leather, covered in places by chainmail and small metal plates. The Orcish workmanship is very distinctive. I ask her what she's doing here. 'Are you hiding from See-ath the Elf again?'

'Of course not. I'm over that now.' Makri lowers her voice, although with the sound of trundling wagon wheels and marching feet all around, there's not much chance of being overheard. 'I'm worried about this visit to the Vitin oracle. I don't like it. It's dangerous.'

'I don't like it either. Lisutaris shouldn't be going out on a secret mission with only a few followers.'

'I tried to dissuade her,' says Makri. 'She got angry and told me to drop the subject.'

'It seems like the Vitin Oracle is too important to the Sorcerers Guild for her to ignore.'

'Why?'

'I don't know. Maybe they all still worship the Goddess Vitina. Or maybe they really need some advice from the oracle.'

'I don't believe anyone can foretell the future.'

I agree with Makri. 'I've always regarded these oracles as frauds. Either they give you some prediction so general it could mean anything, or so obscure there's no telling what it means.'

Makri looks up, scanning the skies above, as if for dragons. We ride on in silence for a while.

'Where did you find another set of Orcish armour?'

'The King's armoury.'

'You didn't consider wearing normal, human armour?'

'I like this better.'

'It's guaranteed to annoy some people.'

'You mean Elves?'

'I was thinking more of the Niojans.'

'Bishop-General Ritari and Legate Apiroi don't like me anyway. I don't think they like Lisutaris much either. They're tolerating her as War Leader because of the Elves, but I don't trust them. What if they make trouble when we meet up with the Simnians?'

58

'I can't see that happening. By that time we'll be ready to face the Orcs. You can't change War Leader at the last moment.'

'It's another reason Lisutaris shouldn't be visiting this Oracle. If Legate Apiroi hears about it, he'll be down on her like a bad spell.'

'We'll just have to— I stop talking as Makri suddenly vanishes through the canvas flap, disappearing into the wagon. I ride on for a while. All around the army is moving forwards, slowly but relentlessly. After a few minutes I poke my head through the flap.

'I thought you said you were over See-ath?'

'I lied.'

'He's out of sight now.'

Makri re-emerges.

'I wish he'd stop taking messages to Lisutaris. Why do the Elves have to send her so many messages?'

Chapter Nine

Next day I waken long before dawn. Wakening myself at any hour is a talent I learned a long time again. As long as I haven't drunk too much beer the night before, it usually works. I dress quietly, place my new Elvish sword in its scabbard, and slip out of the wagon. The night is dark, the moons hidden by clouds. The only light to guide me through the mass of tents and wagons comes from the distant torches at the southern sentry outpost. Whenever the army camps, several pathways are left clear for access. I pick my way through the tents till I reach the path that runs south, then hurry along towards the sentry post. My cloak is wrapped around me and I have a hood over my head, something I very rarely wear. Out of the corner of my eye I notice another figure moving, parallel to me, but I pay no attention. I haven't told my unit I'm leaving. I left a note saying I was called away suddenly and will be back in a day or so. Anumaris will know where I've gone but she'll keep it quiet. Four heavily armed guards and an officer are huddled round a brazier at the checkpoint. The night is chilly, as they often are in these open farmlands.

'Identify yourself,' says the officer, softly.

'The password is future days,' I respond, deliberately not giving my name or rank. The officer nods, and waves me through. I keep my head down as I leave, not wanting to be recognised by any casual observer. Before I'm out of earshot I hear a familiar voice behind me being challenged by the guards, and giving the appropriate response. I walk on into the darkness. I have a fine illuminated staff strapped to my back. I could use it to make light, but I don't. We're trying to leave as unobtrusively as possible. I walk south, following the track made by the army's horses and wagons. After travelling a few hundred yards I come upon a group of four people and seven horses. Each of the group is swathed in a cloak, their faces hidden by their hoods.

'Captain,' mutters Lisutaris.

'Commander,' I reply, keeping my voice low.

Another hooded figure hands me the reins of a horse. I recognise Makri from the way she moves, though she remains silent.

'Captain,' whispers Lisutaris, to Hanama, who I knew was following along silently behind me. Hanama also takes the reins of a horse, a smaller animal than the one that will be carrying me.

'That's everyone,' says Coranius the Grinder, recognisable by his gruff voice. 'Let's be off.' He puts one foot in his stirrup to mount his horse.

'There's one more,' I say.

'What?' Lisutaris is surprised, though she keeps her voice low.

'Last minute change of plan. I invited Gurd.'

'You weren't meant to tell anyone!'

'As your Chief Security Officer I decided we needed another sword. You can trust Gurd.'

'This is an unnecessary risk,' comes a female voice I don't recognise. It must be Ibella Hailstorm, the Abelasian sorcerer.

Gurd arrives, emerging silently from the gloom. He can move very quietly for a large man. Lisutaris stares at him for a few seconds.

'Fine,' she says. 'Let's go.'

We mount up and ride off as quietly as we can. Our secret journey to the Oracle has begun. Very few people know we've left, and none of them know our destination. Lisutaris and Ibella ride in front. We give the camp a wide berth, then turn north-east. The dark countryside is mostly featureless but Lisutaris has assured us she knows the way. We're looking for a small stream which runs down from a hilly area to the east. If we follow that into the uplands, it will take us to the Vitin Oracle. Apparently it's not difficult to reach. The path that leads to it runs through a forest, but it's been well-travelled by pilgrims through the years. We should be there by mid afternoon. Although the oracles have been condemned by the True Church, they haven't actually been made illegal, apart from those in Nioj. What we'll find there, and whether anyone will be expecting us, I'm not certain.

The first faint traces of dawn are appearing as we reach the small river. Lisutaris and Ibella halt for a few moments. My horse, a fine sturdy beast, whinnies loudly then sticks its face in the water, drinking deeply. It's a while since I've ridden any distance, but I'm an experienced enough rider. Unlike Makri, who never rode in her days as an Orcish gladiator, and still doesn't look that comfortable on a horse. The terrain is a little wilder as we head into the hills, leaving the farmland behind. There's a well-defined path but it's become overgrown through lack of use. Bushes crowd in on either side. I spur my horse on till I catch up with Lisutaris.

'If this path becomes any more overgrown there's only going to be room to ride in single file. I'll lead the way from here. Makri, you ride behind me. Gurd, take up the rear. Hanama, go with him. Commander Lisutaris, stay between Coranius and Ibella.'

'Since when did we take orders from you?' demands Hanama.

'Since I became Chief Security Officer of the Commander's Personal Security Unit.'

Hanama scowls at me but no one else objects. I'm faintly surprised to find that Lisutaris actually takes my advice. We set off again. Though it's now late morning, not much light filters down through the overhanging trees. The path ahead is dark. The undergrowth pushes in at us, brushing the horses' flanks. I don't like this. It seems like an excellent place for an ambush. The War Leader of the west shouldn't be in such a vulnerable position. We've taken care to keep our journey secret but I'm wary. I haven't forgotten how easily Deeziz the Unseen got the better of us in Turai. I curse silently to myself. We shouldn't be making this expedition. Oracles are never any good. They're not worth risking your life over.

We ride along in silence. Each of us is alert. I don't know what spells the sorcerers might have in place at the moment, but I hope they've got something to warn us of approaching enemies. If they haven't, we're certainly not going to see them coming, not with the thick forest crowding in on us. None of us is wearing heavy armour. The steel breastplate I'd wear going into battle isn't suitable for riding long distances. It's too heavy. I find myself wondering if the leather shirt I have on would keep out an arrow. Possibly. It wouldn't keep out a crossbow bolt.

The thickly wooded area is oddly quiet as we pass through. I'd have expected more in the way of bird calls and animal noises. We travel along in complete silence apart from the soft regular footfalls of our horses. We're still ascending, though the hills aren't steep. The river, now little more than a stream, is on our right, hidden by the undergrowth. On our left is a thick bank of bushes, thorns and overhanging tree branches. I'm wondering if Lisutaris recognises where we are. It all looks the same to me. Eventually we come to a statue beside the path. It's old, and partially overgrown. A female figure. A Goddess, perhaps, though I don't recognise her. Thinking it might be a landmark that Lisutaris knows, I hold up my hand, bringing us to a halt. I turn towards Lisutaris.

'How far?'

'Less than a mile.'

'Who's the statue?'

'Vitina. Goddess of knowledge and wisdom.'

Vitina. Her entire cult was disparaged and deprecated by the True Church before I was born. I think she might once have been worshipped in Turai, but if she was, her statues and temples have long been removed, or taken over by the church. Nothing remains of her there, apart from some references in a few old books and scrolls in the imperial library.

'Was the path always this overgrown?'

'No,' says Lisutaris. 'It used to be clearer. These days the priestesses don't mind if the way is difficult.'

'Why not?'

'They don't want to be bothered by hostile religious fanatics. In Nioj, Vitina's temple was burned to the ground.'

Heartened by the knowledge that we're almost there, I pick up the pace. I'm keen to get out of this undergrowth. I wonder how long Lisutaris, Coranius and Ibella will need to spend at the Oracle. I suppose there will be some sort of ceremony to go through before they consult the High Priestess, or whoever it is they're meant to consult. I'll be pleased when it's all over and we're safely back at camp.

We pass several more statues. Some resemble the figure of the Goddess Vitina we passed earlier, some are of different female figures. Ancient stone, well carved, though now showing signs of erosion from age and weather. When we suddenly emerge from the narrow path into a clearing I breath a sigh of relief. I wouldn't say we were safe but at least we can't be taken by surprise. Ahead of us is a temple, larger than I was expecting, made of white marble. It's a fine construction, with six large pillars in front of the portico. The marble is clean, undamaged, and well-preserved. Unlike the statues we passed, it shows no sign of age. Someone has obviously been maintaining it through the years. As we approach, a solitary figure walks towards us, a young woman in an ornate blue robe. Her head is uncovered and her dark hair is unusually long, longer even than Makri's. I bring our column to a halt.

The young woman glances at me for only a second or two, without displaying any great interest. She looks past me towards Lisutaris. Though the sorcerer's features are still covered, she recognises her.

'Welcome, Lisutaris, Mistress of the Sky. The High Priestess of Vitina is expecting you.'

Lisutaris slips smoothly from her mount. I've noticed she's an excellent horsewoman. She probably grew up surrounded by horses, and learned to ride as part of her education. Coranius follows her. He's a pale man, with sandy hair, neither tall nor imposing in stature. There's little about his looks to suggest the great power he wields. Like Lisutaris, he comes from the upper classes of Turanian society. Though unlike her, not from the very highest ranks. The cream of our aristocracy rather frowns on their sons and daughters engaging in the profession of sorcery. Lisutaris is something of an exception in that regard, coming, as she does, from an extremely aristocratic background.

Ibella dismounts next, less elegantly. I don't know where she stands in the social classes of Abelasi. Probably, like Coranius, from a comfortable and respectable background, somewhere below the highest ranks. Personally, I'm firmly rooted in the lower classes. Even my name is lower class. Only gentlemen of rank have *ius* at the end of their name. A name ending in *ax* or *ox* marks you from birth as one of the common herd. These distinctions were very important in Turai. Even now that the city has fallen, they're still important. Sons of the aristocracy get all the best positions: there will be very few officers in the Turanian regiments who are not well-born.

I'm expecting to wait outside the temple but Lisutaris motions for me to follow.

'I'd rather stay here and keep watch.'

'Everyone in the visiting party enters the temple,' says Lisutaris.

'We should leave someone on guard.'

'There's no need,' says the long-haired young woman in the fancy robe. 'The Goddess Vitina protects this area.'

'What's she like against heavily-armed Orcs?'

'The Goddess Vitina protects this area,' she repeats.

Lisutaris motions to me again. I shrug, and follow her inside. Everyone lowers their hoods as we enter, as a mark of respect. I follow along, but I'm not pleased at this development. We should have left someone outside, on guard.

'I don't like this,' I whisper to Makri.

'Neither do I,' she whispers back, but whether that's because she fears an ambush, or because she's never that comfortable inside religious buildings, I'm not sure. Makri is a heathen when it comes right down to it, with no respect for our Gods, or any Gods. She'll probably get it in the neck from some divinity one day.

We find ourselves in a high, vaulted chamber. For a temple in the middle of nowhere, it's an impressive piece of architecture. Everything is made of white marble. Good quality material, I'd say, probably as good as the stone used for the King's imperial palace in Turai, and he spent a lot on that. There are several marble statues, a few made of bronze, and, beneath a huge shrine at the back of the room, a life-size gold representation of the Goddess Vitina. Arrayed around the walls are bronze shields, silver plates, gold drinking cups and plenty of other expensive items. I'm not certain what they represent. Offerings from past visitors, perhaps? It's an impressive sight. This is obviously not one of those religions that doesn't like to display its wealth. I wonder who keeps them safe these days? So much precious metal must be an attractive target for bandits, out here in this isolated area. Maybe the Goddess Vitina really does protect the place. Or perhaps the Sorcerers Guild offers them some discreet assistance.

I study the statue. The Goddess Vitina is portrayed with a peaceful face and very long hair, like the woman who greeted us, and the two others who stand waiting. One of them, an elderly, grey-haired woman, is wearing possibly the fanciest cloak I've ever seen. It's purple and red, elaborately embroidered, and edged with gold. A cloak like that would cost a fortune, but the price would be insignificant compared to the cost of her necklace, which is made up of several thick gold chains, each decorated by rows of diamonds and queenstone. I'm rather startled by the sight. It's such a heavy-looking item I'm surprised she can walk.

Not only can the High Priestess walk, for an elderly woman she's very upright. She waits in silence as Lisutaris and Ibella approach. Both sorcerers bow to her. I'm surprised by the apparent reverence with which Lisutaris does this. I've never seen Lisutaris actually be reverent to anyone before.

'It is good of you to visit,' says the High Priestess. She has a clear, strong voice.

'I would not pass up the opportunity, High Priestess.'

'I appreciate it's difficult for you these days.'

Lisutaris produces something from inside her cloak. Her purse, which, I recall, contains a magic pocket.

'I've brought you an offering from the Sorcerers Guild.'

'There was no need.'

'We feel the need, High Priestess.'

If I was surprised at proceedings so far, it's nothing to what I feel when Lisutaris starts emptying gold out of her purse. The magic pocket inside her purse is effectively limitless in volume. You can fit anything in there, and it takes up no space and weighs nothing till you bring it out again. Lisutaris starts hauling out thousand-guran gold bars, laying them at the High Priestess's feet. The Priestess watches this quite calmly, as if it's the most natural thing in the world. As the pile mounts, my amazement grows. Just how much money does the Sorcerers Guild give to this place? Apart from the thousand-guran bars, there's a large bundle of gold coins, a good-sized pile of assorted jewels, a ceremonial tripod made of gold, several silver tiaras, a few gold crowns and even a small gold statue.

I glance round at Gurd and Makri, both of whom also seem startled at the sight of the wealth pouring from Lisutaris's purse to lie at the Priestess's feet. When the process finally comes to an end, the High Priestess smiles, quite faintly. Much more faintly than I would if someone had just given me such a huge pile of gold, silver and jewels.

'You are very generous.'

'We revere the Goddess Vitina, this oracle, and you, High Priestess.'

Lisutaris bows again, as does Ibella. I think you could safely say that Lisutaris wasn't quite telling the truth when she said she had a vague interest in the old religion. Number one devotee might be nearer the mark.

The High Priestess has taken all this calmly, though I'm sure there's a glint in the eye of the junior priestess beside her. I can't blame her. It's a hefty bundle of cash. The junior priestess picks up a silver chalice from an ornate, gilded table. She hands it to the High Priestess.

'I know you have little time to spare, Lisutaris, now you are War Leader,' says the High Priestess. 'Do you wish to consult the wisdom of the Goddess?'

'Yes, High Priestess.'

We finally seem to be getting down to business. I'm curious about the procedure, though a little uneasy. If it involves a lot of religious singing and dancing, I'm not going to enjoy it. If we have to chant anything, Makri will really hate it. I wonder what Makri and I are doing here anyway. And Hanama and Gurd. We're just the hired help. We didn't come to consult anyone.

'Should we wait outside?' I venture.

The elderly High Priestess looks at me for the first time. 'The oracle is for everyone.'

'It's all right, we just came along to escort–'

'The oracle is for everyone,' she repeats, ending the conversation.

Beside me, Gurd is looking ill at ease. The Northern Barbarian is not keen on sorcery at the best of times, and he's uncomfortable at the thought of being included in any sort of magical goings on. I'm not that keen either, though I wonder if I could turn it to my advantage. Might the priestess be able to point me in the direction of some winners at the chariot races? I believe the race meeting in Simnia is still going ahead, despite the war.

Four of us - Makri, Hanama, Gurd and myself - have been hanging back. The priestess of Vitina motions for us to advance, which we do, slowly.

Makri whispers in my ear. 'I don't believe in oracles.'

'Neither do I. Unless they say something good. But they never say anything good.'

We find ourselves organised in to a loose line in front of the priestess.

'Do we have to pay for this?' I ask. 'I didn't bring any money.'

Lisutaris shoots me a hostile glance. I glare back at her. She might be in the midst of some religious fervour with her favourite Goddess but I didn't sign up for any oracles. I refuse to be browbeaten into revering a temple which has obviously been raking in the cash for years from gullible customers. I'm still staggered at the pile of gold Lisutaris handed over.

'Please remain silent for the High Priestess,' says her assistant. We fall silent. The High Priestess, resplendent in her robe, looks down the line, taking in every one of us. She sips from the silver chalice in her hand. I'm half-expecting her to go into a trance and start shouting out prophesies but she seems quite calm as she takes a few steps towards us. Not frothing at the mouth or anything. She halts in front of Hanama. The assassin, not a tall woman, looks up at her calmly enough.

'Much death,' says the High Priestess.

She steps over to Gurd, and looks him in the eye.

'Much life.'

Gurd looks relieved. Whatever that means, it doesn't sound too bad. The Priestess halts again, in front of Ibella.

'Fear only poison.'

The High Priestess turns towards Makri, and pauses. She stares at Makri for quite a long time, as if she's not sure what to make of her. Understandable I suppose. Makri's weird make up would probably be confusing for any respectable Priestess.

'Fortunate or unfortunate queen,' she says, finally.

I suppress a snort of derision at the thought of Makri being any sort of queen. My faith in this oracle is diminishing fast and it wasn't that great to begin with. I wish she'd just give Lisutaris her prophesy so we could get out of here. She arrives in front of Coranius the Grinder. He's a famously bad-tempered and impatient man, but he seems quite placid in this environment. It just goes to show how completely the Sorcerers Guild has fallen under the spell of this cult. Gullible, you might say.

'Glorious ending.'

Coranius doesn't react, though it doesn't sound like the greatest oracle a man could have. Depends on when the ending comes, I suppose. Throughout all this, I've been edging back, hoping that the High Priestess might just ignore me. Perhaps if I let her see I'm really not the sort of man who enjoys an oracle she'll just pass me by. Unfortunately, she halts in front of me. I don't like the look in her eye. I think she might have it in for me for asking if we had to pay. She glances at me for only a few seconds, and come out with the following.

'You will throw down your shield and flee.'

'What?'

She turns to leave.

'What's that supposed to mean? I demand. 'Are you calling me a coward?'

'Silence in this temple!' cries Lisutaris, angrily.

'But she said–'

'Silence!'

I glare balefully at our War Leader, and at the back of the High Priestess as she walks away. How dare she give me such an insulting oracle. I'll have a few sharp words to say about this farce when we're outside.

The priestess finally approaches Lisutaris. I suppose she's been saving this for her big finish. Oracles always love a bit of suspense. Charlatans, all of them. She stares at Lisutaris for a few moments. For the first time, the High Priestess's eyes close. She stands with her eyes closed for thirty seconds or so. Finally she opens them.

'The Goddess Vitina has something of great importance to say to you, Lisutaris, Mistress of the Sky.'

We wait, impatiently in my case.

'But it is not yet time. Her oracle will be transmitted to you at the appropriate moment.'

I'm astonished, and only just manage to avoid laughing. Lisutaris drags us out here on this foolish mission, hands over a huge pile of gold, and she doesn't even get a prophesy? Absolutely ridiculous. I'm half-expecting Lisutaris to complain. You'd think she had good reason to. Unfortunately, all that happens is that the sorcerer bows her head respectfully.

'Thank you for your attentions, High Priestess.'

'You are welcome, Lisutaris, Mistress of the Sky. And you are welcome to visit this temple at any time.'

I'll bet she is, if she's bringing a magic pocket full of gold. I'm disgusted with the whole thing. *You will throw down your shield and flee.* An outrageous slander. I'm not going to let that pass by unchallenged. We troop silently out of the temple. Outside, the recriminations begin right away. Lisutaris gets in first.

'Is there no end to your boorish behaviour? How dare you speak disrespectfully to the High priestess!'

'What? You heard what she said to me! "You will throw down your shield and flee!" I've never been so insulted in my life!'

'You've been insulted far worse,' rages Lisutaris. 'Did you fail to notice how important this expedition was to me? Is it impossible for you to show respect for others?'

'Not when they're accusing me of cowardice! What's the matter with you and the rest of the Sorcerers Guild? How much gold have you given that old fraud over the years?'

Lisutaris's eyes blaze. It's probably not a great idea to annoy such a powerful sorcerer as Lisutaris. I'm wearing a good spell-protection charm round my neck, woven from red Elvish cloth, but it's not strong enough to deflect an angry spell from the Head of the Sorcerers Guild. Very few things are strong enough to do that. Nonetheless, I refuse to back down.

'This whole enterprise has been a dangerous waste of time. If we get ambushed and killed on the way back, don't blame me.'

'It was not a waste of time,' says Ibella.

'Really? Lisutaris didn't even get an oracle!'

'It will be transmitted at the appropriate time,' says Lisutaris.

I laugh. 'I notice the High Priestess didn't mention that before you handed over the cash. If I was paying that much I'd expect quicker results.'

'The High Priestess is not answerable to you!' cries Lisutaris, furiously.

'Seems like she's not answerable to anyone. Has it not struck any of you that these were the worst oracles ever? No insight whatsoever. She said "much death" to Hanama. How much prophetic power did that require? Hanama's an assassin! Hardly a brilliant piece of fortune telling, was it?'

'I took it as an interesting insight,' says Hanama, stiffly.

'I liked my oracle,' says Gurd.

'That's because she said "much life" to you! Anyone would like that when they're going to war. Doesn't mean the woman has any power of telling the future. As for Makri, "fortunate or unfortunate queen?" Some chance.'

Lisutaris takes a stride towards me. 'Captain Thraxas. I'm ordering you to be quiet.'

Lisutaris is of course, my commanding officer. She can order me to be quiet. Here, on this secret mission, I wasn't expecting her to. I stare at her.

'Very good, Commander,' I say.

'I've got a glorious ending to look forward to,' grunts Coranius. From his tone, it's impossible to tell what he thinks about that prediction. 'We should be going.'

It's late afternoon. I clamber on my horse, less gracefully than I'd have liked. The atmosphere among us is bad. Lisutaris is still furious, and I'm about as angry as a troll with a toothache. Nonetheless, it's still my responsibility to lead us back to camp. I turn in my saddle to check that we're lined up in the correct order. 'Move out,' I say, and we head away from the temple. Behind me I hear Ibella talking to Lisutaris.

'The Priestess told me to fear only poison. Not so bad, in the circumstances.'

'Have you properly applied my Spell of Resisting Poison?' asks Lisutaris.

'Yes.'

'Then you're protected from all known harmful substances. Make sure you maintain the spell.'

That sounds like a useful piece of sorcery. It's not on offer to me. Many of the Sorcerers Guild's most powerful spells are only given out to the most important members of the army, and the highest ranking diplomats. They don't have the power to protect everyone. We pass out of the temple courtyard, through the clearing, and back into the clinging undergrowth. We're immediately plunged into near-darkness from the weight of vegetation above and around us. It suits my mood. I hate oracles.

Chapter Ten

It seems darker on the return journey. Perhaps the afternoon sky has clouded over, though the canopy of trees reaching over the narrow path makes it impossible to tell. We travel in silence, broken only by a bird cawing somewhere in the forest, a sound that rapidly becomes irritating. I try and forget my annoyance and concentrate on getting us back to our base camp as swiftly as possible. I still have a very bad feeling about this mission, and I trust my feelings. They've helped me survive through many campaigns. I don't like the noisy squawking from the unseen bird. It stops. I don't like that either. I hold up my hand, bringing us to a halt, then dismount and squeeze my way past the others till I'm standing next to Lisutaris. She asks me why we've halted.

'Someone's watching us.'

Lisutaris turns her head, scanning each side of the pathway. 'I can't sense anyone.'

'I can.'

'Let me check.' Coranius the Grinder holds up his hand and mutters a few words. After a few seconds there's a faint flash of light.

'What was that?'

'Standard scanning spell. I can't sense anyone nearby. We're alone in this forest.'

'I don't think we are. I don't like the way that bird went silent.'

'Maybe it's having its dinner,' says Coranius, with some degree of sarcasm.

Lisutaris frowns. I'm not her favourite person at the moment, but she doesn't dismiss my concern out of hand. She speaks a few words in some ancient language. 'I've scanned the area too,' she says, seconds later. 'I didn't pick up anyone either.' Lisutaris never seems to need much preparation to perform her spells. They just happen instantly. It's impressive. That doesn't mean she's always right.

'Can we move along?' comes Hanama's voice, from the rear of the column. 'There's no point wasting time here.'

73

'I'd listen to Thraxas,' says Gurd. 'I've marched through a lot of forests with him. He can recognise danger.'

I ask Lisutaris if she can put up some sort of sorcerous protection around our group. 'I don't want someone firing a crossbow bolt into you.'

'It wouldn't touch me,' replies the sorcerer.

'It might if it comes with a spell attached. You're not invulnerable.'

'I'm aware of that,' says Lisutaris. 'But it's not easy to maintain a barrier while we're moving. If I put up defences, it will slow us down, and we're short of time.'

'Time which we're wasting here,' grunts Coranius. 'There's no one around.'

The Head of the Sorcerers Guild scans the trees again, then turns back towards me. 'Are you quite sure this is necessary?'

'Yes. We're in danger.'

Lisutaris nods. 'Ibella, protect our right. Coranius, the left. I'll protect the front and the rear.'

'Really?' Ibella Hailstorm isn't pleased. 'In this terrain? We'll be slowed down to a crawl. It will take us hours to get out of here.'

'Do as I say,' Lisutaris tells her. Ibella and Coranius start muttering spells to put up a defence on each side. There's a slight but noticeable drop in temperature as their sorcery comes into effect. A barely visible blueish light now extends along side our column on each side. Lisutaris does the same, taking on herself the more difficult task of maintaining a barrier in front and rear, a barrier which has to be constantly moved as we progress.

'Makri, get close to the Commander and stay there.'

Makri nudges her horse towards the sorcerer. I squeeze my way along to my horse, mounting it with difficulty in the confined space. We set off, now travelling much more slowly. Ahead of me I can see the faint blue light of Lisutaris's barrier and I make sure I don't get ahead of it. No doubt the rest of the party think I'm a fool but I don't care. It's my responsibility to look after our War Leader.

We ride like this for around half an hour, without incident. Even so, I still have the feeling we're being watched. Ibella mutters to Coranius that maintaining the sorcerous barrier is tedious and unnecessary. As soon as she finishes her complaint there's a great flash of yellow light. blinding in the gloom of the forest. The yellow light changes to green as it hits Ibella's barrier on our right. For a fraction of a second it seems as if there's an almost physical struggle between the two intangible forces.

'Hold the barrier!' yells Coranius. Next thing I know there's a dart heading for my face. I duck. There's a fierce rattling sound all around. When I look up, a multitude of darts are crashing and rebounding off our defensive walls. My sword is in my hand but with the flashing lights, darts everywhere, and our enemy concealed somewhere in the trees, it's impossible to know where to attack. Makri has positioned herself right in front of Lisutaris. I think Lisutaris has reinforced Ibella's barrier, holding off the darts, but in the confusion it's hard to tell what's happening. As another flash of light erupts on our flank, I catch a glimpse of a shadowy figure in the undergrowth.

'Gurd!' I scream. 'To me!'

Gurd leaps from his horse. I do the same, and we prepare to plunge into the trees. I shout at Makri and Hanama, telling them to stay where they are. At that moment there's a burst of purple light, brighter than any that have gone before. This time it's coming from our party. It blasts into the trees with such force that branches are ripped off and the air is filled with whirling twigs and leaves. Somewhere in the distance there might be a scream, unless it's just the birds. There's a moment's silence. I look round. Lisutaris is standing in her stirrups, her hand still outstretched from casting whatever dread spell she just sent into the forest. Her eyes have turned completely purple, and a few purple sparks are still flickering around her fingers. There are no more spells or darts flying at us. Whoever our attacker was, Lisutaris seems to have repelled them.

'Let's move!' I shout. and start getting back on my horse.

'Wait,' cries Coranius.

I turn my head angrily. 'We have to—' My voice tails off as I see Coranius holding the limp figure of Ibella Hailstorm in his arms. Lisutaris shakes her head to clear it. After casting such a powerful spell, even a sorcerer like Lisutaris can take a few seconds to recover her normal senses.

'What is it?'

'Ibella. She's dead.'

'What?'

I force my way along the line. Coranius is still holding the Abelasian sorcerer's limp frame. The only wound I can see is a small dart in her shoulder.

'What? How?'

Coranius studies the wound. 'Poison,' he says.

'You said she was immune to poison!'

'Not this poison, apparently.'

Lisutaris curses loudly. She dismounts, and puts her hands on Ibella, checking for signs of life. From her distressed expression it's obvious that Ibella really is dead.

'We have to go,' I say, loudly. 'Right now. Put Ibella's body on her horse and we'll get out of here. Gurd, back to the rear of the column. Makri, stay with Lisutaris. Lisutaris and Coranius, get your barrier up again.'

'I can't,' says Lisutaris. 'Not yet. I've used that spell and I'll need to learn it again.'

Even our most powerful sorcerers can't keep an infinite number of spells in their minds. If Lisutaris has fully used up her barrier spell she'll need to refresh herself from her grimoire before she can use it again.

'Then we'd better move quickly and hope for the best,' I say. 'I'll tie Ibella's body to her saddle.'

'No need,' says Coranius the Grinder. He places her back on her horse, lifting her quite easily. Physically, as well as magically, he's stronger than he looks. He intones a brief spell, still touching the body.

'She'll stay in place now.'

'Fine. Let's go.'

We mount up quickly and move on, traveling as fast as we can in the confined space. The expedition has turned into exactly the disaster I feared. A waste of time at the Oracle, and one of our sorcerers dead. If there's another powerful attacker waiting for us further along the path we could lose Lisutaris and probably the war before we've even left Samsarina.

After we've ridden for another ten minutes or so, I notice there's a little more light filtering through the trees. We're coming out of the densest part of the forest. The path begins to widen. My leather tunic is scratched and torn from twigs and thorns from the cloying undergrowth and I have a few scratches on my face, but we're almost out of it now. When we find ourselves back at the point at which the thick woods give way to grassy slopes I breath a sigh of relief, though I don't let my guard down. We ride downhill for almost a mile. No one speaks. Eventually I raise my hand, bringing us to a halt under a small copse of trees. It's now evening. I ride back a few yards towards Lisutaris.

'We're about a mile from the camp. We'll be running into the outlying sentries soon. We planned to drift back into camp in ones and twos to avoid attention but now we've got a dead sorcerer with us. What would you suggest?'

Ibella hailstorm is still propped up on her horse, held there by Coranius's spell. It's going to be difficult to explain. Lisutaris hesitates.

'Could you animate her?' suggests Hanama. 'Make her look alive?'

'No. And that's a distasteful suggestion.'

'If you ride back into camp with an obviously dead companion someone will notice. You can't trust all the sentries to keep quiet about it.'

'What else can I do? I'm not going to be able to keep Ibella's death a secret. Her Abelasian colleagues are probably already wondering where she's gone.'

'Are you still intent on keeping it secret that you visited the Oracle?' asks Hanama.

'Yes.' Lisutaris is insistent. 'That can't be known. The Niojans just wouldn't stand for it, and we need them.'

'Surely you and Coranius have enough spells between you to get her back into camp without any of the sentries noticing her? You'll still have to explain her death to your officers but at least the troops won't see her.'

'I suppose we could do that. We could carry her in the magic space.' Lisutaris doesn't sound enthusiastic. Not surprising, I suppose, as it involves walking into the camp with her dead friend hidden in her purse.

'Who attacked us?' asks Gurd.

'Deeziz the Unseen,' I reply.

'You don't know that for certain,' protests Coranius.

'Who else would have the power to fight you, Lisutaris, and Ibella? And kill Ibella with a poisoned dart when you're all supposed to be immune to poison?'

'We are immune,' says Lisutaris. 'To every poison known to sorcery, herbalism and biology.'

'It seems that Deeziz the Unseen knows some things about poison that we don't.' Coranius is once again grim. As he directs these words towards Lisutaris, I notice a hint of accusation in his voice.

'Apparently she does.' Lisutaris scowls. 'Thraxas is right. It can only have been her. No one else could disguise her presence so completely from our detection spells. That means the most dangerous Orcish sorcerer is right in our midst. She's somewhere close enough to know our plans, even the most secret.'

'How could she possibly know we were going to the Oracle?' wonders Coranius.

'I'd guess that's she's in our camp, using the identity of someone we trust,' I say.

'Isn't it your job to find her?'

'Yes. So far I haven't. But I did keep us alive along enough to have another attempt.'

We dismount close to the camp. In the darkening evening we can see the torches at the sentry posts and the camp fires within. Gurd dismounts and walks alongside me. He has a few scratches on his face but is otherwise unharmed.

'That didn't go so well,' he says.

'I knew we shouldn't have wasted our time visiting an oracle.'

'You won't be saying that when I'm queen,' says Makri, a few paces behind us.

'Queen of where?'

'Who knows? Somewhere good, I hope.'

'I wouldn't pin your hopes on it. That High Priestess was a fraud. Look what she said about me. Throw down my shield and flee. Outrageous accusation. I've spent twenty five years protecting Turai and I've never fled yet.'

'She did get it right about Ibella Hailstorm. Warned her about poison. And what happened? About an hour later she was dead from poison. Gurd, you'd better watch out. The oracle thinks Thraxas is losing his nerve. Probably disappear from the battlefield at the first sight of an Orc.'

'I'm going to be fighting an Orc in about fifteen seconds if you keep on like this.'

'Are you calling me an Orc?' demands Makri.

We separate before reaching the camp, arriving in ones and twos, maintaining our secrecy for now. I catch up with Gurd once we're safely inside.

'Will Tanrose be cooking tonight? I need something hearty.'

'No time for that,' says Lisutaris, appearing out of the gloom. 'I need you for a meeting in my tent.'

'Am I meant to starve to death?'

'If necessary. Be there in ten minutes.'

Lisutaris hurries off. Makri follows at her heels.

'She's not that great a War Leader,' I tell Gurd. 'Everyone knows you have to give your best warriors time to eat.'

Gurd laughs. He promises to save me some stew, then heads off to his unit.

Chapter Eleven

I'm not in the best of moods as I approach Lisutaris's command post, a large rectangular tent with enough room for tables, chairs and maps. I've been insulted by an Oracle and denied sufficient food, both high up on the list of things I don't enjoy. Not only that, I've witnessed an important sorcerer lose her life for no good reason. If I'd had time for more than a single flagon of ale I might be tempted to give our War Leader a piece of my mind. I might do that anyway.

Inside the tent Lisutaris is already in conference with her commanders - General Hemistos, Bishop-General Ritari and Lord Kalith-ar-Yil. As a guard ushers me in, she's in the middle of an awkward conversation.

'The death of Ibella Hailstorm is very unfortunate,' says General Hemistos. 'She was one of the west's more powerful sorcerers.'

'I still don't understand why you were so far from our camp, on a secret mission without our knowledge,' adds Bishop-General Ritari. The Niojan looks expectantly at Lisutaris, waiting for an answer. Demanding an answer, perhaps. Niojans are always suspicious. Lisutaris can't admit the truth, particularly to Ritari. She hesitates.

'I was responsible,' I announce.

'You?'

'As Chief Security Officer for our War Leader I learned of a powerful sorcerous threat. It was my recommendation that Lisutaris deal with the matter personally, with a small group of helpers. Which she did, very effectively. Unfortunately, Ibella didn't survive. Nonetheless, the mission was a great success, eliminating the threat.'

'Are we going to learn details of this threat?'

'I've advised against it. It's best that as few people as possible know about it. For security reasons.'

'What security reasons?' demands Ritari.

'Reasons that can't be mentioned. I take full responsibility.'

Having argued them to an impasse, I allow Lisutaris to take it from there.

'Captain Thraxas is right,' she says. 'The matter is best kept private. I'll inform you of any new developments. And now gentlemen, I must confer in private with my Chief of Security. I'll see you tomorrow before we march.'

'I'm not happy about information being withheld,' says Bishop-General Ritari. 'Nioj will not be kept in the dark about important war matters.'

I wouldn't say that either Hemistos, Ritari or Kalith regard me with much warmth as they exit the tent. No General likes being told by a Captain that something is private. The Bishop-General takes the time to cast a further unfriendly glare at Makri, who's been waiting silently in the background.

'Thanks for that,' says Lisutaris, after they've gone. 'Ritari was suspicious and I was having trouble diverting him. We'll be meeting up with the Niojan army soon and that has to go smoothly.'

'Is there any chance the Bishop-General would actually refuse to allow the Niojan army to join us?'

Lisutaris doesn't think so. 'The Bishop-General isn't friendly but he is keen to fight. Legate Apiroi is more of a problem. I have the impression that Apiroi would like to take over from Ritari. He's been hinting that he should be on my command council. They're both sending reports back to King Lamachus and I doubt that Legate Apiroi is painting me in a good light.'

King Lamachus of Nioj is known for his hostility toward Turai. Not that the Niojans really like any other country that much. They're a hostile nation. It wouldn't take much for our alliance to fall apart, even in the face of an Orcish invasion.

'We simply can't give the Niojans an excuse to leave the alliance. Captain Hanama's intelligence suggests that Apiroi might recommend that, if it helped him in his power struggle with the Bishop-General.'

'We can't fight the Orcs without the Niojans.'

'I know,' says Lisutaris. 'Make sure no one learns of our visit to the oracle. That would really harm my position.'

'We shouldn't have gone.'

'The Sorcerers Guild required it. As I fully explained.'

81

'I maintain it was a waste of time. Furthermore –'

'If you're about to complain about what the High Priestess said about you, don't bother. The High Priestess is never wrong. Look what happened to poor Ibella.'

'But she didn't even give you a prediction! You went all that way for nothing.'

'It was not for nothing, Captain Thraxas. If the High Priestess said my oracle will arrive at the appropriate time, then it will.'

'I still think–'

'I'm not interested in what you think,' says Lisutaris, brusquely. 'Not about the Oracle anyway. I'd still be annoyed with you for your rudeness to the High Priestess if it wasn't for your good work on the way back. I didn't sense the danger, and you did. If we hadn't set up barriers, things could have been a lot worse. I thought that with the attention I've given to my detection spells, I'd have some idea that Deeziz was close. I was wrong.'

Lisutaris takes a thazis stick from her purse and lights it, something she's been doing less of recently. 'I don't have to tell you how serious this is.'

'I know. She could mount another attack at any moment. How did this Orcish woman become so powerful? Western sorcerers have always had the upper hand.'

Lisutaris shrugs. 'Who knows? Maybe she really did spend ten years meditating on a mountaintop. Ten years which I spent at balls and parties, as she was quick to point out when we met in Turai.'

'I wouldn't say that was fair,' says Makri. 'You didn't spend all your time at balls and parties. Although you did throw a grand ball every year. And you went to a lot of parties. But I'm sure you practiced your sorcery as well.'

'Thank you Makri.'

'I suppose there were a lot of dances at the Palace. But really, you had to go to them. You couldn't refuse invitations from the Royal Family. It's not your fault you couldn't practice as much as Deeziz.'

'Yes, thank you Makri. Now, if we could move on from discussing my inadequacies, perhaps we could think of a plan? We can't go on like this, we need to find Deeziz.'

Lisutaris looks at me. I remain silent.

'Captain Thraxas? I'm waiting for suggestions.'

'I know. But I don't have any. My staff are still checking up on peoples' backgrounds, trying to find out if there are any inconsistencies, gaps in their history, time unaccounted for.'

'That would be excellent if we were checking references for a new Professor at the University,' says Lisutaris. 'But we're not. We're looking for the most dangerous sorcerer in the world, a sorcerer who is about to wreck our campaign before we even get started. You have to think of something better.'

'I haven't come up with anything.'

'I thought you were good at this sort of thing?'

'I'm sharp as an Elf's ear. But I still haven't come up with anything.

A messenger hurries in, hands a note to Lisutaris, and hurries out again. She reads it quickly. 'The sorcerers from the Abelasian Guild will be here in a few minutes. I have to talk to them about Ibella.'

I ask Lisutaris if she has time for a word about Tirini Snake Smiter.

'Not really. Why?'

'Saabril Clearwater asked me to visit her. She's in a bad way and not getting better.'

Lisutaris, who already has plenty to worry about, looks almost hopeless for a moment. She shakes her head sadly. 'I know. I tried to help but nothing I did was any use.'

'Is Saabril Clearwater any good?'

'She's the best medical sorcerer available. She arrived with two sorcerers from Kastlin whom I know well, and they speak very highly of her. She patched one of them up on the way here, after a horse-riding accident.'

'Tirini said "they took my shoes." Does that mean anything to you?'

'Not really. Of course, Tirini was famously fond of shoes.'

'I know. But she seemed fixated on it. Did she have one particular pair of shoes that were important to her?'

'Not as far as I know. She had hundreds of pairs.'

'Could her sorcerous power be bound up in one particular pair? If she lost them might it make her ill?'

Lisutaris hesitates. 'Well...it's not completely impossible for a sorcerer like Tirini to put some of her power into an inanimate object. No one would do it with shoes though. It would normally be done with a wand, or perhaps a weapon, like a sword.'

'Maybe Tirini did it with her shoes.'

'I really don't think she did, Thraxas. I've seen her wear a hundred different pairs in the course of a month, and her power never diminished. Even if she had put some of her sorcery into a pair of shoes, for whatever reason, their loss wouldn't kill her. She'd still get better.'

A guard pokes his head into the tent. 'The Abelasian sorcerers are here, Commander.'

Lisutaris acknowledges him, then turns back to me. 'Captain Thraxas, find Deeziz the Unseen. That's why I hired you.'

I exit the tent, wondering how the success of the war effort suddenly landed on my shoulders. I only ever claimed to be a good man in a phalanx. I never said anything about outwitting the world's most cunning sorcerer. It's not something I'd have put myself forward for. Outside, I find myself in the midst of an altercation between two sentries and Legate Apiroi. The Niojan official is attempting to enter the tent and the sentries are keeping him out.

'Commander's orders. No one is to enter.'

'Then why is this Turanian Captain leaving?' Legate Apiroi manages to put a lot of dislike into the words *Turanian Captain*.

'I was invited,' I inform him. 'Unlike you.'

'And what would our Commander want with you?'

'Vital war work. Private, of course.'

The Legate's black uniform is in pristine condition, as is the rest of his equipment. He doesn't have the look of a man who's familiar with the battlefield. I know from the background checks my staff did that he doesn't have much of a war record. Unlike Bishop-

General Ritari, who's an experienced soldier, Legate Apiroi is more of a politician.

'What's this I hear about our War Leader leaving the camp on a secret mission, on your advice?'

'Once again, Legate, it's private. You're either inside Lisutaris's inner circle, or you're not. You, it would seem, are not.'

The Legate steps closer to me. He's a muscular figure, with a thick neck beneath his closely cropped hair. 'If our War Leader's inner circle is full of meddling incompetents like you, I give little for our chances against the Orcs. What bad advice have you been giving our Commander? What foolish mission did you send her on?'

'None of your business.'

'A powerful sorcerer died. That makes it my business. I'm here to make sure Niojan lives are not wasted by poor leadership.'

I place a hand on his chest and push him back. I put a lot of force into it but it only moves him a few inches.

'Put your hand on me again, Turanian dog, and I'll gut you.'

'Threaten me again and I'll run you through.'

'I'll have something to say about this in my next communication with King Lamachus.'

'Fine. Enjoy your talk. I'm off to do important war work.'

I stroll off. Behind me, the Legate is again demanding entry to Lisutaris's tent, and the sentries are keeping him out. The Legate's an important man, but the sentries are more worried about offending Lisutaris than they are about offending him, which is sensible. I'm on my way back to my wagon to check up on my unit when Makri catches up with me.

'Lisutaris asked me to leave while she meets the Abelasian sorcerers. I don't think they want me there while they talk about their secret religion. Did you know they had a secret religion?'

'Yes. But I didn't realise it was so important to them.'

'Why does Lisutaris revere that High Priestess so much?'

I can't answer that. I don't remember ever revering anybody.

'I saw you arguing with Legate Apiroi.'

'He's an angry man. He doesn't like Turanians.'

'He hates me,' says Makri.

85

I can imagine what the Legate thinks of Makri, and don't contradict her. We walk by many campfires. Soldiers' eyes follow Makri as she passes. She's quite a well-known figure these days.

'Are you any nearer to finding Deeziz?'

I admit I'm not.

Makri frowns. 'We can't go on like this. How can we plan anything if she's right here, spying on us?'

'It's a problem.'

'Have you ever been in a campaign where there's an enemy sorcerer in your camp?'

'No. Usually our own sorcerers would pick it up. It's just unfortunate that Deeziz is so good at hiding herself.'

'What are you going to do?'

'I don't know.'

'But you're chief security officer. Why aren't you more worried?'

'Because I'm hungry. I'm concentrating on that.'

'Well as long as you've got enough pies inside you when Deeziz destroys our army, we've nothing to worry about,' says Makri. When she first arrived in Turai I'm sure she didn't even know what sarcasm was. The city can be very corrupting.

'Makri, I'm sensing a certain lack of faith in my capabilities.'

'You just said you had no idea what to do!'

I come to a halt, and turn to my quarter-Orc, quarter-Elf, half-Human companion. 'That's true. But that doesn't mean I won't come up with something. It's just a matter of time.'

'How much time?'

'I don't know. But I'll come up with something. I always have in the past. And when I do, make sure you're ready.'

'For what?'

'For swift action. You remember that Orcish sorcerer who appeared when we were at the chariot races? He was firing spells all over the place until I beat him over the head with a chair. That put an end to his activities. Take note of that. Even the most powerful sorcerer can be vulnerable when they're engaged in sorcery. They tend not to notice people sneaking up behind them with a hefty piece of furniture in their hands. That's why we have the Sorcerers Auxiliary Regiment to protect our own. So if the time comes when I expose Deeziz, you make sure you're ready.'

'To hit her with a chair?'

'Yes. Or stab her. Whichever's easier.'

When I reach my wagon, Droo greets me enthusiastically. Anumaris and Rinderan express concern about my absence.

'Secret business for the War Leader,' I tell them.

'Did you visit the–'

'Don't ask. It was secret. Don't mention it again.'

Anumaris isn't satisfied. 'Couldn't you have given us some warning you were leaving?'

'Then it wouldn't have been secret. Did any of you learn anything useful while I was away?'

Rinderan takes a notepad from beneath his cloak and reads. 'All of Lord Kalith-ar-Yil's staff can give a full account of their time previous to arriving in Samsarina. No reasons to suspect any of them. Lord Kalith however, still has a period that can't be accounted for. There are no independent witnesses to confirm his claim that he was engaged in solitary religious duties for his people.'

Anumaris consults her own notepad. 'Hanama and her intelligence staff all seem to be above suspicion, apart from an Elvish woman she's engaged as her assistant. This woman, Megleth, refuses to provide us with any details of her past whereabouts. Hanama also refuses to provide any information about her.'

'Where does she come from? What's she doing on Hanama's staff?'

Anumaris doesn't know. Apparently Hanama refuses to even discuss her.

'That's not very satisfactory,' I say. 'Lisutaris's intelligence chief can't be employing mysterious Elves and refusing to tell us anything about them. I'll make enquiries. Anything else?'

'We also have some suspicions about Bishop-General Ritari's second in command, Legate Apiroi. He was sent by the Niojan command to assist Ritari, but he didn't travel with the Bishop-

General and his journey took two days longer than it should have. The Legate can't, or won't, account for this.'

'Was there anyone with him?'

'No, he travelled alone.'

'Interesting. Legate Apiroi is exactly the sort of trouble-maker you might expect to be an Orcish spy. Throwing his weight around, calling people Turanian dogs for no reason. I've been suspicious of him since we met. Keep working on him.'

I turn to Droo, and ask the young Elf if she's managed to investigate anything.

'I investigated plenty of things! I've been all round the army checking up on mysterious singers. You know, like Moolifi you told us about.'

'Did you discover anything?'

'The Samsarinan infantry are all issued with two bottles of beer a day as part of their rations. Not such a large amount I suppose, though it is good beer. The cavalry get a small bottle of wine each. I tried it, it's good wine. The Turanians mostly drink whatever beer they can find. They were running short because the refugees didn't bring a lot with them, but Lisutaris managed to find them a supply so they're all a lot happier now. The archers from Kastlin drink wine but they've got a few bottles of klee with them. I've never tried that before, it's strong. I wonder if we could make it on Avula? The Abelasian sorcerers brought a barrel of–'

Anumaris Thunderbolt interrupts her. 'Did you find out anything apart from the drinking habits of the army?'

'Like what?'

'Like mysterious singers or entertainers. That's what you said you were looking for.'

'Oh. Right. No I didn't find anything like that.'

'You've completely wasted your time!' cries Anumaris.

This seems harsh to me. I was enjoying Droo's intelligence report. 'Keep at it,' I tell her. 'You never know what information might come in useful. I'll be interested in any beer, wine or klee-related stories.'

Droo beams, pleased. Anumaris and Rinderan look very unimpressed.

'I want to check out some more people. Saabril Clearwater, sorcerer from Kamara. She arrived with two sorcerers from Kastlin. They're all working close to Lisutaris, see if there's anything suspicious about them. Also, keep your ears open for any mysterious shoe-related stories.'

'Shoes?'

'Tirini Snake Smiter claims someone took her shoes. What the significance of this is, I don't know, but I'm interested.'

'Yes Captain,' say Anumaris and Rinderan. Neither of them look very interested.

'How are our provisions? Can either of you two sorcerers produce a meal instantly? I've hardly had a chance to eat for forty eight hours.'

'I'll light the fire.' says Anumaris. Lighting fires when necessary is one of the perks of being a sorcerer. Watching Anumaris bring our campfire to life with a spell reminds me of Tirini doing the same thing, back in the Avenging Axe when it was cold in winter. I can remember the pained expression on her face, as if using sorcery for such a menial task was beneath her. She was disgusted at being obliged to stay in a tavern in Twelve Seas, and didn't waste any opportunity to remind everyone what a low-class dive it was.

We have a decent enough supper. It's not on the level of Tanrose's cooking, but it'll keep me going for a while. Makri appears. She could eat with the other members of the Sorcerers Auxiliary regiment who make up Lisutaris's staff, but I don't think she feels comfortable with them. She sometimes joins us at our campfire, always keeping one eye on the command tent, in case she's needed.

'Do you think Cicerius is alive?' she asks, after a while.

'Probably not. I doubt he'd have been able to escape from Turai.'

Makri frowns. 'He was with us in the Avenging Axe when the Orcs arrived. Didn't you see what happened to him?'

I shake my head. 'I blacked out when Deeziz used that spell. He wasn't there when I came round. No one was.'

Makri thinks about this. 'If he's dead do you think they might try and stop me going to the university?'

'I don't know. I suppose it depends who ends up in charge of the city.'

Makri's frown deepens. I know why she's worried. She has an overwhelming ambition to attend the university in Turai. This ambition was undimmed by the fact that the university did not accept female students, nor anyone with Orcish blood. It seemed like a hopeless endeavour, even though Makri had gained the requisite qualification at the guild college. As it transpired, she preformed such sterling service for Turai that Deputy-Consul Cicerius promised he'd persuade the Senate to allow her to attend.

'Plenty of people heard him promise,' she says. 'You were there, and Lisutaris. And Coranius.' A touch of doubt enters her voice. 'They could tell whoever ends up in charge that Cicerius said I could go, right?'

There was a time when I'd have mocked Makri's ambition. Now I don't. Makri deserves support on this one. She's earned her place.

'Lisutaris will support you,' I tell her. 'So will I. Whatever the next government of Turai is, I'll make sure they know the Deputy Consul promised you could go to the university. And I'll make sure they keep their promise.'

I drink some wine to wash down the last of my food. 'You've even got the money now, after all the loot we won in Elath.' Thanks to the unparalleled brilliance of my betting campaign, Makri, Lisutaris and I all ended up winning more than ten thousand gurans, gambling on Makri's progress in the great sword fighting tournament, money which is at this moment nestling comfortably in Lisutaris's magic purse. It's my turn to frown. 'Unless Lisutaris handed it over to The High Priestess.'

'I'm sure she wouldn't have.'

'I hope not. She was certainly keen to make her a rich woman.'

When night falls, and I lie down to sleep in the wagon, I find myself thinking about Tirini's shoes. That shouldn't be my main concern. Finding Deeziz is the important thing at the moment. But I'm still thinking about the missing shoes. There's something strange about it, though I've no idea what.

Chapter Twelve

It takes us another two days to complete our rendezvous with the Simnian army. Both days pass uneventfully. That doesn't stop me from worrying about Deeziz the Unseen. There's no telling what her next move will be. For those of us aware of her presence, it adds a whole new level of anxiety to the already stressful business of going to war. Reports from Makri suggest that Lisutaris's thazis intake is on the rise.

'It wouldn't be so bad if I had proper access to beer,' I tell Makri. 'But the Sorcerers Auxiliary Regiment is sadly under-supplied. It's a bad oversight on Lisutaris's part. It makes you wonder if she's fit for the job.'

I stare rather mournfully at the empty tankard in my hand. 'I've completely run out, and that corrupt fool of a quartermaster refuses to hand over any of tomorrow's supply in advance. How am I supposed to function like this? It's no wonder I can't catch Deeziz. If I was back in Turai I'd be full of beer by now, probably slumped happily on my couch.'

'That never really helped with your investigations,' says Makri.

'Of course it helped.'

'Only in your imagination.'

'It wouldn't be so bad if wasn't for that prig Anumaris. I was half-way through concocting a promising scheme with Droo for purloining extra supplies when she butted in and started lecturing us about our duties. As if snatching a little extra beer was going to harm the war effort. I'm starting to loathe the woman.'

'She's efficient and does everything properly,' says Makri. 'You should be pleased to have her.'

I glare at Makri. 'I'm not taking lectures from a woman who's currently hiding in my wagon because her Elvish ex-lover is delivering messages to our War Leader.'

'Keep your voice down. He's close, he might hear us.'

'How long is this going to go on for?'

'Until the war ends and the Elves all go back home. Or I get killed. Either one.'

'You're going to have to face him some time.'

'No I'm not.'

'Yes you are.'

'No, I'm really not going to do that,' says Makri. 'I'm going to keep hiding till it's all over. I can never face See-ath again and that's all there is to it. Also I'm never having a lover again. Probably I won't talk to any Elves either, just to be safe.'

'What if you're guarding Lisutaris at some vital moment and he appears? Are you going to run away?'

'I'm hoping that doesn't happen.'

I shake my head, and peer out of the flap. See-ath is disappearing in the opposite direction. I tell Makri he's gone. She sits up.

'I should never have become involved with an Elf.'

'Getting involved wasn't the problem. It was the death threats afterwards that made the situation awkward. Does your wish never to talk to Elves again extend to female Elves?'

'I'm not sure. Why?'

'Because I've been meaning to question Hanama about her new Elvish companion. An unknown woman with an unknown past. Not the sort of person who should be close to Lisutaris, given our present difficulties. Come with me.'

'Why?'

'Normally I can't exchange more than a word with Hanama without us getting into an argument. She likes you, maybe that will help.'

'Are you sure See-ath has gone?'

'Quite sure.'

'What if he comes back? Did he look like he was coming back?'

'Makri, please stop this. Let's go and visit our so-called Chief of Intelligence.'

We leave the wagon. We're now on the southern border of Simnia, and the Simnian army has met us as arranged, on time and in good order. Accompanying them are various units from the territories to the north of Simnia, including some from Gurd's homeland. There are strange accents to be heard all over the enlarged camp, and, unfortunately, a lot of Simnians.

'I've never liked Simnians.'

'That's the hundredth time I've heard you say that,' says Makri.

'It bears repeating.'

'I think it was the first thing I ever heard you say, when I first arrived in Turai. Followed by "Can you buy me a beer?"'

Makri comes to a halt, and scowls. 'I just remembered the third thing you said.'

'Which was?'

'"If you can't buy me a beer then take your pointy ears somewhere else, pointy-eared wench."'

'Forthright and to the point. I was toughening you up for city life.'

Hanama and her Intelligence Unit are quartered in a series of small, plain tents, pitched on the far side of Lisutaris's large command tent. We pick our way through the guards, whose numbers have increased since our experience at the Oracle.

'Are you really suspicious of this Elvish woman? Or are you just looking for an excuse to criticise Hanama?'

'Both. She shouldn't be introducing strange Elves into our ranks. And she deserves criticism. She's an assassin. I don't believe she has any loyalty to anyone except the Assassins Guild. If Lisutaris thinks she can really trust her she's making a mistake.'

'I trust Hanama,' says Makri.

'She'd kill you without a second thought if her guild accepted a commission for the job.'

'Maybe. Maybe not.'

As we arrive, Hanama is sitting cross-legged on her own, in front of her tent. She regards me with no apparent emotion but she smiles when she sees Makri. The assassin's smile doesn't light up her face, though it does make her look even younger.

'Hello Makri, I've been meditating. Would you like some food?'

Makri politely declines. She never has much of an appetite. Hanama seems disappointed. I'm mildly offended that she didn't offer me any food, not that I'd have taken it from an assassin anyway.

'Who is this Elvish woman you've employed?' I demand, getting straight to the point.

Hanama rises smoothly to her feet. She's a small woman, several inches shorter than me, and about one quarter as wide.

'Why do you ask?'

'Because anyone working close to Lisutaris needs to be checked out. She might be a security risk.'

'She isn't.'

'That's for me to decide.'

'No it isn't.'

'Yes it is, Captain Hanama. Kindly provide me with full details so I can do my job.'

'Her name is Megleth and she's an Elf,' says Hanama. 'That's all I can tell you.'

We stare at each other.

'I demand to know more.'

'That's all I'm saying.'

'I outrank you.'

'No you don't, we're both Captains.'

'I outrank you in this. I'm Captain in charge of security.'

'You don't outrank me in anything,' says Hanama, coldly. 'Commander Lisutaris is already aware of Megleth.'

'I don't believe you.'

'I have no interest in what you believe.'

As always, when faced with Hanama, I feel a mixture of annoyance and distaste. I loathe assassins.

'So where is this mysterious Elf?'

'With Commander Lisutaris.'

'She's with Lisutaris?' I turn to Makri. 'Why have you left Lisutaris alone? Hanama's Elf is probably assassinating her at this moment.'

'Lisutaris told me to leave. She had private business to discuss.' Makri wrinkles her brow. 'I don't like when she does that.'

'Neither do I. We should check she's safe.'

'You're being ridiculous,' says Hanama. 'There is no danger.'

At that moment the sky goes dark, there's a flash of lightening and an enormous peal of thunder. Rain begins to pour down in torrents from a sky which was clear only seconds before. A gale-force wind blows through the camp, driving the rain before it, picking up debris from the ground and tossing it around. So unexpected is the storm, and so violent, that for a second or two I'm disorientated, not sure what to do. I snap out of it quickly as another deafening clap of thunder explodes overhead.

'Makri!' I scream to make myself heard. 'This storm isn't natural! We need to get to Lisutaris.'

The storm can only have been conjured up by a hostile sorcerer. It came out of nowhere, and it's the wrong season for bad weather in Samsarina. Makri and I hurry towards the command tent. Though it's been raining for only a few minutes the ground is already treacherous. So heavy is the rain that the earth turns to mud beneath our feet, and water laps up over our ankles. With the wind howling in our faces, progress is slow. By the time we're close to Lisutaris's tent we're wading through several inches of mud. My face is sore from the pounding rain, some of which is now turning to hailstones.

All around us, tent pegs are torn out of the ground by the wind. Soldiers struggle to hold on to their tents which threaten to fly away in the gale. Items of clothing, food, even weapons, are picked up by the storm and whirl around our heads. It's a chaotic scene. A horse gallops past, panicked by the ferocity of the storm, knocking down a centurion who ends up in a pool of muddy water. His soldiers drag him out of the pool and look for cover, but there's no cover to be had. We're stuck on an open plain in the middle of a storm as bad as any I've ever encountered.

Outside Lisutaris's tent, the sentries are still at their posts though they're struggling to stay on their feet. One soldier's helmet blows off and he falls over in the mud trying to catch it. I'm finding it difficult to advance. My weight - which I refuse to admit is a handicap in most circumstances - does make it difficult to pass quickly over the cloying mud. Makri sprints ahead of me, reaching Lisutaris's tent just in time to see it collapse. The large, square edifice tumbles in on itself, engulfing its contents and anyone who was inside. As I catch up, Makri is attempting to lift it, a hopeless endeavour given the size of the canvas, now water-logged and extremely heavy. With the wind and hailstones battering us we make no progress at all. While we're still puzzling about how to proceed, the tent begins to rise in the air. Not flapping furiously, like all the other tents currently careering all over the place, but serenely. I take a step back. The tent comes to a halt about ten feet in the air. Standing beneath it is Lisutaris. She moves one of her fingers slightly, causing the tent to descend gently and land behind her.

'What is happening?' she asks.

'Sudden severe storm probably of sorcerous origin,' I reply.

The Head of the Sorcerers Guild scowls. She looks up. Lightning flashes in the sky, producing more deafening thunder. 'This is irritating,' she says. 'So much for my afternoon nap.'

The driving rain has already reduced Lisutaris's nicely-coiffured hair to a stringy mass dripping over her shoulders. Her sodden cloak flaps around her ankles. Becoming annoyed with this, she snaps her fingers. A faint purple light appears above her head, acting as an umbrella, diverting the rainwater to each side of her. That's a useful spell. Makri and I both step into the dry patch.

'Can you stop the storm? I yell. 'It's going to wash the army way at this rate.'

'I have sorcerers to prevent this sort of thing happening,' declares Lisutaris. 'Where are they?'

A bedraggled sorcerer hoves into view, struggling against the elements, mud and water splashing round his feet as he approaches. He stumbles up to Lisutaris and makes an attempt to salute.

'Habintenat Cloud-Controller, Senior Storm Class Sorcerer, Weather Unit, Sorcerer's Regiment, Samsarinan Division,' he says. Which, in the circumstances, is quite a lengthy introduction.

'Well, Habintenat Cloud-Controller, what happened? You're supposed to look after the weather.'

'We were overwhelmed by a sudden hostile spell, Commander. It's like nothing we've encountered before. We couldn't fight it. The rest of the Weather Unit is still trying.'

Lisutaris is displeased. 'You should be ready for anything. You're meant to save me from wasting power on this sort of thing.'

'Sorry Commander. The spell is extremely potent.'

The unfortunate Habintenat, completely drenched and looking very sorry for himself, isn't exaggerating. Whatever spell has caused this storm is certainly potent. A sudden gust of wind sends Makri careering into me, and she looks embarrassed to have lost her footing. She draws her sword and tries to pretend it didn't happen.

'Take a few steps back,' says Lisutaris. We step back into the driving rain. I drag my sodden cloak over my head to protect myself from a barrage of hailstones. Lisutaris holds one hand in the air, but pauses, her brow wrinkling in concentration. She hesitates for a few seconds, as if judging the correct response. She's still frowning slightly as she holds up her other arm. Her eyes turn purple and purple light begins to flicker around her hands, both signs that she's using a major piece of sorcery. She chants something in one of the arcane languages beloved by the Sorcerers Guild. The chant goes on for around ten seconds, which is longer than most of the spells I've heard Lisutaris use. As she finishes chanting, the rain begins to ease off. I risk emerging from beneath my cloak. The hailstones have stopped and the wind is dropping. There are no more flashes of lightning. The rain drops to a light drizzle, then halts completely.

Our War Leader is looking thoughtful. 'That was indeed a potent storm spell. Sorcerer Habintenat, return to your unit and assist with drying operations. When you've done that bring your unit back here so I can teach them how to look after the weather properly.'

Senior Storm Class sorcerer Habintenat salutes, then departs, squelching his way through thick mud and puddles. Where only half an hour ago there were rows of neatly laid out tents, there are now nothing but fields of ruined, drenched canvas. Wagons have sunk up to their axles in the mud. Horses whinny as they try to shake themselves dry, and soldiers wander around looking confused. By this time Lisutaris's young aide-de-camp Julius has arrived and an array of junior officers and young sorcerers are gathering round the wreckage of the command tent. Lisutaris barks out instructions to her messengers, telling them to summon her commanding officers and her senior sorcerers. They depart as quickly as they can, which is not all that quickly, given the mud, water and general chaos. There's a moment of silence. I shiver as water runs down my neck.

'I'm as wet as a mermaid's blanket.'

'We all are, Captain Thraxas.' Lisutaris looks down at her rainbow cloak with some disgust. 'This is ruined. I really should have put a waterproofing spell on it. I wasn't expecting a storm. No one was. Our weather unit is meant to prevent enemy sorcerers from attacking us this way.'

'Are you sure it was sorcery?' asks Makri.

'Quite sure. It was a weather spell more powerful than I've ever encountered this far inland. Producing so much rain without easy access to the sea or a nearby lake is very difficult.'

All three of us, Lisutaris, Makri and I, have our hair hanging round our frames as if we've just been dragged from the ocean. It's a funny sight, in a way, though I decide not to mention it.

'Captain Thraxas. This simply cannot go on. Look at the chaos everywhere. This storm will delay our march for a day or more and may well make us late for our rendezvous with the Niojans. Deeziz the Unseen is somewhere nearby and I want her found. You're my Personal Chief of Security, so find her. Find her quickly or I'll appoint someone else who can.

'I'm doing my best.' That sounds limp as soon as I say it.

'Then your best isn't good enough. I've heard you bragging about your investigating prowess often enough. It's time to show some results.'

'I've been—'

'Drinking mainly, from what I hear,' growls Lisutaris, who's too wet and angry to listen to anything I have to say. 'I'd have replaced you already if I wasn't trying to keep it secret that Deeziz is here.'

'We came here looking for Megleth, Commander,' says Makri, something I'd almost forgotten.

'The Elf? Why?'

'Captain Thraxas thought she might be assassinating you.'

'Captain Thraxas should spend more time on his own duties.'

'Captain Hanama refuses to give me any information about her, Commander. I need to know more, for security reasons.'

'Megleth does not require checking,' says Lisutaris.

'Who is she and what's she doing?'

'Forget Megleth. Find Deeziz. If the army learns we're in danger from an Orcish sorcerer it will be a disaster.'

A loud splashing noise nearby alerts us to the arrival of Legate Apiroi. He arrives looking surprisingly dry, though his boots are covered in mud.

'Commander Lisutaris,' he says, loudly. 'What's this I hear about an Orcish sorcerer? Rumours are spreading that Deeziz the Unseen is among is! Is this true?'

'Absolute nonsense!' says Lisutaris.

'People are saying she caused the storm!'

'Then people are mistaken. Weather anomalies will happen, Legate.'

Lisutaris shoots me a murderous look, the meaning of which is quite clear. Find Deeziz the Unseen or say goodbye to my position as Chief Security Officer. I withdraw swiftly. Makri follows me a little way through the mud.

'Shouldn't you be looking after our War Leader?'

'I'm keeping her in sight,' says Makri. 'I'm just withdrawing a few yards till her temper cools.'

'Has she been criticising you too?'

Makri nods, and looks glum 'Yesterday she criticised me for making too much noise when she was trying to think. I was only practising with my swords. I need to do that every day.'

Makri has one Elvish sword, bright silver, beautifully made. The other is her black Orcish blade, a foul-looking weapon which seems to suck in light rather than reflect it. Most people would regard it as an ill-omened weapon. The Niojan Bishop-General would probably regard it as sacrilegious even to draw it from its scabbard in his presence.

'I've been working hard on this investigation,' I tell Makri. 'Not that Lisutaris appreciates it. It's outrageous for her to insult me. I rescued her from Turai!'

'As you never tire of pointing out.'

'The stress is getting to her. She can't cope. A good War Leader doesn't let her temper blind her to the fine qualities of her staff, particularly Captain Thraxas, warrior of Turai.'

'Did you know Kublinos has been walking around with a pretty Elvish sorcerer?'

I'm confused by the sudden change of topic. 'Kublinos?'

'The Harbour sorcerer from the Port of Orosis.'

'I know who you mean. What about him?'

'He was courting Lisutaris quite strongly back in Elath.'

'So what? Lisutaris wasn't interested in him.'

'I know. But now he's met this Elf from the Elvish sorcerers Regiment and he's been going round everywhere with her, and bringing her to sorcerers' meetings.'

'So what?'

'I think it might have contributed to Lisutaris being in a bad mood.'

I stare blankly at Makri. 'Why would that put her in a bad mood?'

'Because Kublinos is walking around with a pretty Elvish sorcerer.'

'But Lisutaris wasn't interested in him.'

'That doesn't mean she wants to see him just forget about her immediately and meet up with someone else. It's insulting.'

'Why is it insulting?'

'He should have been sad for longer after Lisutaris rejected him.'

'That doesn't make sense!'

'Yes it does,' insists Makri. 'He should have been sad for longer, instead of grabbing hold of the first pretty Elf who came along. Now it looks like being rejected by Lisutaris didn't mean anything.'

I feel a desperate urge for beer. I look around, just in case a bottle or two might be floating past in the rivers of mud, but there's none in sight.

'I don't think she likes Kublinos flaunting his new woman at sorcerers' meetings,' says Makri.

I'm convinced she's talking nonsense. 'How could you know this? Aren't you, by your own admission, completely hopeless at everything to do with romance?'

'Only my own romances. I can see what's going on with other people.'

'And you're saying this is contributing to Lisutaris's bad mood?'

'I think so.'

'Well that's great. Now we're really doomed. Not only is our War Leader bested at every turn by a superior Orcish sorcerer, she's also sulking like a schoolgirl because her boyfriend doesn't like her anymore. I tell you Makri, this is what happens when you put women in charge. I knew it was a mistake. Lisutaris probably can't cope with Deeziz because she's too busy fashioning love charms to make Kublinos jealous. The west is going down in flames because Lisutaris is sulking about a man she didn't even like in the first place. We should never have made her War Leader. She'd be better off looking after Tirini. They could talk about shoes together.'

'Now you're being ridiculous. And I don't like you insulting women.'

'Really? You're no better. How many vital messages from the Elves have we missed because you've been skulking around, hiding from See-ath?'

'None.'

'That's what you say. It wouldn't surprise me if you've destroyed the entire line of communication between Lisutaris and the Elvish command. It's a scandal that brave warriors like myself should be brought to ruin by a bunch of women who can't think about anything else except lovers and shoes. I'm going to see Gurd for some proper wartime discussion about killing Orcs.'

'And drinking beer?'

'Some beer may be drunk.'

'If you get drunk Lisutaris will hear about it and you'll be in trouble.'

'Lisutaris will be too busy sobbing in her tent about Kublinos to notice.'

Makri returns to her position as bodyguard. I trudge off through the mud in search of Gurd, beer, and some manly conversation. I find him and a few other Turanian soldiers re-erecting their tents. They've almost accomplished this, working quickly and efficiently. The sun has emerged and steam rises from the sodden canvas. I clap my old companion on the shoulder. 'Reminds me of the time these Simnians attacked us in the marshlands. We showed them how to fight, wet or dry.'

I pause, waiting for Gurd to take up the story. It's one of our favourites. We must have told and re-told it hundreds of times in the Avenging Axe. Gurd doesn't oblige. He seems distracted. He walks over to the remnants of his cooking fire. I follow him, and try again.

'You remember we were holding them off and suddenly our centurion shouted "There's an alligator behind us?" That made everyone jump!'

I roar with laughter. Gurd doesn't laugh.

'Is there something the matter?' I enquire. 'And do you have any beer?'

Gurd drags a small bottle of beer from his bag of supplies and hands it over. 'Nothing's the matter.'

'Then why didn't you laugh when I reminded you about the alligator?'

'I've heard that story hundreds of times. I've told it myself hundreds of times.'

'So what? The Simnians and the alligator is one of our best stories. We always laugh.'

Gurd starts poking around moodily in the remains of the fire, looking for sticks dry enough to light.

'Damn it Gurd, what's the matter? I came here looking for some hearty conversation between old soldiers and you're plodding round like a broody mare. You wouldn't believe the nonsense I have to put up with Lisutaris and Makri. I'm getting desperate for some proper conversation. Anything will do as long as it doesn't involve women.'

Gurd looks up at me. 'Tanrose wants to have a baby.'

I'm so startled by this I almost let go of my beer, though not quite.

'A baby? Now? In the middle of the war?'

'She wants to start now. Hopefully the war will be over before it arrives.'

I struggle to repel the wave of depression that threatens to envelop me. I came looking for Gurd to get away from Makri and her girlish chatter, and now I'm having a conversation about babies with my oldest fighting companion. It wouldn't have happened when I was a young man. Turai is finished. The west is doomed. My immediate inclination is to finish my beer and flee, but such is my regard for Gurd, I know I can't. I'm trapped. With any luck, he won't ask for my opinion.

'What do you think?' asks Gurd.

'Eh…'

'It doesn't seem like the best time, I know. I thought we'd wait till after the war, when we were married. But what if I don't survive? At least I'd have a child for Tanrose to remember me by. I have no children, Thraxas. A man should have offspring. Tanrose is keen. She's not at an age where she can wait much longer.'

The story of our fight with the Simnians, carried out in difficult circumstances in marshland, with alligators threatening, is a fantastic story. I desperately wish I was telling it now. I struggle to think what to say to Gurd.

'Well, if you want a baby, I suppose you'd be as well starting now. The war isn't going to drag on for nine months. We'll be dead or victorious by then.'

Gurd nods. I'm hoping that might be all I'm required to say on the subject - it not being a subject I want to discuss in the first place - but Gurd isn't finished.

'What if I'm not ready? What if I make a poor father? I think we might be rushing things. But if we don't rush things I might get killed in battle and where will Tanrose be then? Do you think we should get married right away? There's a priest in the next cohort, I expect he could do it.'

I cast a stern look at the grey-haired barbarian. 'Gurd, you've known me long enough to realise I can't manage a conversation like this on one small bottle of beer. If you want my advice, you're going to have to bring out the rest of whatever supplies you have hidden away.'

Chapter Thirteen

Offering an opinion on whether someone should or should not have a child is something I'd rather not do. Were it anyone else but Gurd I'd have refused, but a man has certain obligations when he's fought at another man's side. Even so, it's a stressful experience, and it takes me some time to extricate myself. I wouldn't have made it through had Gurd not happened to have secreted away several bottles of ale. I can't help feeling angered. If even a mighty warrior like Gurd is letting himself be distracted by this sort of thing, what chance do we have? You can be sure the Orcish army isn't talking about babies. Nor shoes, I reflect, somewhat bitterly. I keep thinking about Tirini's shoes, and it's annoying me. I'm annoyed at myself for wasting time. I should be concentrating of finding Deeziz. Tirini's shoes are an unwelcome distraction.

I come to a halt. With the mud underfoot and a fair supply of beer inside me, I'm finding it hard going. I notice I'm not far from Tirini's tent. What did she mean, "they took my shoes?" Who took them? Why? Neither Gurd nor Tanrose were able to cast any light on the matter. Tanrose remembered that Tirini was wearing a fancy pair when she whisked them all out of the city. Yellow with pink stitching, and an impractically high heel. The sort of thing Tirini would normally wear. Neither of them could recall what happened to these shoes. Tanrose thinks that when they finally arrived in Samsarina, Tirini was wearing a plain pair of slippers, but couldn't remember where they'd appeared from.

Of course, Tirini might have been carrying any amount of shoes around with her, in a magic pocket, perhaps. It's the sort of thing she'd do. It wouldn't surprise me if she always had a few spare sets of fashionable clothing with her, hidden in the magic space, ready to put on as the occasion demanded. Save her from going home to get changed between fashionable parties. I wonder about her shoes. I wonder why she's still sick. According to Lisutaris and Saabril, her sorcerous attendant, she should have recovered by now. I decide to call in and see how she is.

I find Saabril Clearwater sitting outside Tirini's tent, reading a scroll. The storm doesn't seem to have affected them too badly.

105

Whatever damage was done by the elements has been quickly remedied. Given Saabril's sorcerous power, that shouldn't have been difficult. I wonder if she's had any such success with her patient.

'How's Tirini?'

The young medical sorcerer screws up her face, an expression I take to mean that Tirini is still unwell.

'I'm not making any progress. She won't eat, and she sleeps badly. I'm very worried.' She indicates the scroll she's holding. 'I've been trying to find some alternative treatment from my Kamaran School of Sorcery, but I haven't come up with anything.'

Saabril stands up. 'Whatever happened to her in the magic space seems to have sapped her will to live.'

'Is she actually going to die?'

'It's possible.'

'You're a medical sorcerer. Highly qualified, according to Lisutaris. Why can't you cure her?'

Saabril Clearwater shakes her head. 'I just can't. I don't even know what's wrong with her. Strange things can happen in the magic space.'

'Strange things can happen outside the magic space as well. Has she been attacked by sorcery?'

'No. Or at least, none that I can identify. I brought another medical sorcerer in for a second opinion, one of the Simnians, but he couldn't find anything wrong with her either.'

'I'd like to see her.'

Saabril lifts the tent flap and I walk inside. Tirini is propped up on a camp bed, staring into space. She looks much the same as before. Her hair is lank. Dark roots show beneath the blonde. Her face is becoming increasingly gaunt. It doesn't take a medical expert to realise she can't go on like this for much longer. The combination of not eating, and whatever affected her in the magic space, will carry her off soon. Again, I find the sight upsetting. One of my last memories of Tirini before we left Turai is of her casting scorn on the untidiness and uncleanliness of my rooms at the Avenging Axe. It amazed her that I didn't even have a servant to clean up for me. Now she's not even in a fit state to clean herself, though Saabril has been doing her best to care for her. Saabril does give the impression of being a woman who cares. She has a re-assuring manner, and a soft, pleasant voice.

'Hello Tirini.'

Tirini is staring into space. She doesn't acknowledge me. I raise my voice a little. I'm uncomfortable, trying to question a sick woman. I've interviewed sick people before, in the course of my investigations, but I don't enjoy it.

'I was wondering about your shoes.'

This gets her attention. She looks in my direction, though whether she's quite focusing on me, I can't tell.

'What sort of shoes did you lose? Were they fancy high heels?'

She doesn't reply. I try again. 'Or were they slippers? I heard you had some slippers, when you with Gurd and Tanrose.'

At this, I think I see a faint reaction. Tirini's eyes focus on my face. She struggles to speak.

'College,' she whispers.

'College? What do you mean?'

Tirini's eyes lose their focus again.

'What do you mean, college? Is it something to do with the shoes you lost?'

Tirini sits back, and stares into space. I raise my voice again, to repeat my question, but Saabril Clearwater puts her hand on my arm.

'I don't think she can take any more questions,' she says, softly.

She's right. Tirini Snake Smiter is in no state to answer questions. She's in no state for anything. She'll be dead soon enough if no one finds a way to cure her. We leave the tent. Saabril tells me she's been to see Lisutaris again, hoping for help. Lisutaris hasn't had time to attend personally, but has promised to send medical sorcerers from other units. Sorcery is a very wide field; no one knows every spell, and there are different methods and systems. Perhaps someone will be able to help.

I make my way through the assembled ranks of the Sorcerers Regiment and the Sorcerers Auxiliary Regiment on my way back to my wagon. Most of the army's tents have been repaired, horses retrieved, wagons fixed and so on, but it's cost us a whole day's travelling. We're late for our rendezvous with the Niojans. I'm depressed by my visit to Tirini, though still quite warmed by Gurd's beer. Perhaps because of that, I halt in front of Lisutaris's command tent. I'd like to ask her a few questions. I remember it wasn't that long ago that she was insulting me. I shrug. She's probably over it by now. Even if she's not, I'm used to talking to people who don't want to talk to me. That's what I spend most of my life doing as an investigator.

There are various officers and military delegations waiting to talk to our War Leader. High-ranking Simnian officers, two Elvish commanders, a few senior sorcerers. I push my way to the front of the queue and announce myself.

'Captain Thraxas, Chief Security Officer of the Commander's Personal Security Unit. Urgent business with our War Leader.'

To the annoyance of the assembled officers, the guards let me through. There are hostile mutterings behind me as I stride into the tent. Inside, Lisutaris is sitting at her desk while Makri lurks behind her, being vigilant.

'Captain Thraxas. I wasn't expecting to see you for a while. I'm very busy,' says Lisutaris.

'Important business, Commander. It can't wait.'

'What is it?'

'Can you tell me any more about Tirini?'

'What?'

'Tirini Snake Smiter. I want to know more about her.'

'Why?'

'I'm looking for her shoes.'

Lisutaris drums her fingers on her table, something I don't recall seeing her do before.

'I thought you'd come with news about Deeziz.'

'I need to talk about Tirini.'

'Why?'

'It's important.'

'In what way?'

That's difficult to answer. I don't really know in what way. I just feel that it is.

'Make it quick,' says Lisutaris. 'What do you want to know?'

'Why does she like shoes so much? Was she born rich? Did she grow up in luxury?'

'No. Tirini's father was a minor official at the Palace. Poldius, I think his name was. Respectable, but not wealthy. The same sort of background as a lot of sorcerers.'

I nod. 'When did she start being obsessed with fashion and so on?'

'I think she always has been. Is this actually important?'

'You never know what might be important.'

Lisutaris looks at me rather pointedly. 'I'm starting to think of a few things that might not be.'

'I remember when I dismissed her as useless, back in Turai, you defended her. You said she had a lot of power. Is that true or were you just defending her because she's your friend?'

'She is powerful. She always was, right from her first days at the sorcerers college. That's how she got her name.'

'How?'

'One of their professor's spells went wrong. He accidentally unleashed a mutated, magic snake, causing panic all over the building. It was far too powerful a beast for any of the students to fight. They were all told to stay in their rooms while the professors hunted it down. But Tirini found it in her wardrobe, nibbling on her shoes. Naturally she was furious, and blasted it out of existence. No magical creature can mess around with her footwear. She's always been extremely powerful.'

Lisutaris looks rather sad. 'She's been a good friend too. I hope you can help her, but I really can't spare you any more time. I need to talk to the Elvish officers.'

'When I was talking to Tirini, she said two things. *Someone took her shoes,* and *college.* Did she wear some special sort of shoes at college?'

Lisutaris answers impatiently. 'How would I know that? Tirini is younger than me, she attended the college after I'd left.'

'So you can't tell me any significant shoe-related information about Tirini at college?'

'No, I can't. Are you going to surprise me at the end of this conversation by telling me you've had some inspiration about Deeziz?'

'No.'

Lisutaris glares at me. 'Ensign Makri, if Deeziz kills me, make sure Captain Thraxas is discharged from the army in disgrace and banished from Turai.'

'Yes, Commander.'

Outside the tent, the waiting officers and Elves look at me with disapproval as I walk by, not liking the easy way I gained access to Lisutaris while they're still waiting outside. I walk off, attempting to look like a man on important business, meanwhile wondering what to do next. I should be looking for Deeziz but I've come to a dead end. I'm interested in Tirini's shoes but I need time to ponder my next move. I come to a halt.

'Beer. Of course.'

It's no wonder I've been floundering. You can't expect Thraxas, number one chariot among investigators, to do his job properly if you deny him beer. It simply won't work. I reach my wagon in time to see Anumaris Thunderbolt emerge with her notebook in her hand.

'You're largely responsible,' I tell her.

'What?'

'I'm floundering around here, unable to make progress in this vital investigation. And you know why? Lisutaris's fanatical anti-beer instructions, aided and abetted by the informer she sent to spy on me and report every move. Meaning you. It's all very well you running off to Lisutaris telling tales every time I so much as glance at a flagon of ale but did you ever stop to think how harmful this is to my work? If my investigation fails and Deeziz the Unseen kills Lisutaris, it will be mainly your fault. How does that feel? You'll be remembered in history as the woman responsible for the demise of the west.'

'I do not run off to Lisutaris every time—'

I hold up my hand. 'Enough, Storm Class Sorcerer Anumaris. I'm not going to put up with it any longer. I'm off to find a proper supply of beer and there's nothing you can do about it. Count yourself lucky I don't denounce you to the army. If they knew how you'd been hindering my work they'd probably lynch you. Junior Ensign Droo, where is the nearest easily-accessible supply of ale?'

'The Simnians.'

'I detest Simnians.'

'Their quartermaster brought in eight wagon-loads.'

'Really? Well, we all need to co-operate in times of war. Lead me to him.'

I depart with Droo, heading over to the left flank of the slowly advancing army to investigate the important matter of the Simnian ale supply.

Chapter Fourteen

I've soldiered all over the world. It's therefore not that much of a surprise to find that I know the Simian Quartermaster. Not a good surprise, unfortunately. It must have been twenty years ago that I encountered Calbeshi, campaigning down south in Mattesh. As a young man he was a loud-mouthed braggart and a hopeless soldier. I don't expect he's improved any with the passing years.

'What the hell?' he exclaims, as I approach. 'Is that Thraxas? Haven't they hanged you for cowardice yet?'

'Calbeshi, I might have known you'd find an easy job, far away from the fighting. How much beer have you stolen since you've been quartermaster?'

'Not as much as you've drunk, from the looks of you,' growls Calbeshi. He's large, paunchy, bald and ugly. Much the same as he was when he was young.

'I thought you'd be dead years ago,' he says. 'Probably from an arrow in the back, fleeing from battle.'

'Lucky for you soft Simnians I'm not. I've been fighting Orcs while you've been tucked up safely in bed.'

'And not making a very good job of it. Shame Turai was destroyed. I hear you didn't put up much of a fight.'

'I put up more of a fight than you ever will. It's taken you long enough to get here.'

'I was in no rush. Your army's led by women.' Calbeshi looks at Droo. 'And you've got an Elf. Very sweet. Mind you, she's probably tougher than most Turanians.'

'If you insult my city again I'll run you through.'

Calbeshi laughs. 'Your sword's been rusted in its scabbard for the last ten years, from the looks of you.'

The Quartermaster's platoon have been unloading barrels of beer, prior to distributing them to their regiments, but I notice they've opened one already, tapping it and laying it on the ground where they've been helping themselves. Much as I imagined they would. I glare at Calbeshi. 'Are you going to stand there like the useless Simnian dog you are, or are you going to give me a beer?'

The Simnian raises his eyebrows. 'Why would I do that?'

'Because I saved your hide down in Mattesh. Without me you'd never have got out of the jungle.'

'Without you we'd never have been trapped there in the first place.' Calbeshi takes a leather tankard from a crate. It's a familiar soldier's item - tough and lightweight, impossible to break. He fills it from the open cask and hands it to me.

'Turanian scum,' he says, handing it over.

'Simnian dog,' I reply, raising the tankard. I notice Droo already has a full tankard of her own. I'm not sure how she managed that. Possibly she went and asked for it politely. That would have been another approach, I suppose.

Calbeshi draws himself a beer. 'So, how are things looking?'

'Not that great. The Orcs are better organised than last time, and our army is smaller.'

'What's Lisutaris like as War Leader?'

'Good. She's made us better organised too, which is something. What do the Simnians think of her?'

'Most didn't like it when they heard they'd picked a woman, but there were some that said she can bring down dragons. That's a point in her favour. Can she really do that?'

'She can. Just as well, because the Orcs are controlling them better than ever. They got them flying in winter. I saw her bring down two right in front of the walls.'

'Didn't save your city though, did it?'

'It didn't. But I wouldn't give anyone else much chance of leading us back there.'

I look at my tankard, which is empty. 'I need a refill.'

'We didn't bring this beer all the way here just to fill up fat Turanian bellies.'

'Just give me a refill, Calbeshi, and I won't tell your men about your dishonourable behaviour in Mattesh.'

'Dishonourable behaviour? I was the only man who knew how to fight.'

'For a Simnian, maybe. That's not saying much. Are you ever going to fill this tankard?'

'You ought to take care. This is proper Simnian beer, not that cheap swill you brew in Turai.'

'Simnian beer? You don't know what the word means.'

Calbeshi fills up my tankard, and his. We drink. For a lying, cheating Simnian, I suppose he's not such a bad person.

Droo is perched on the beer wagon with a large flagon in her small hands. 'I met this fool when I was down in Mattesh,' I tell her. 'The other Simnians fled like rabbits, but he managed to hang around, as far as I recall. Once Gurd and I had saved his life four or five times, he almost learned how to use a sword properly.'

Calbeshi roars with laughter. 'Gurd? Now he wasn't bad, for a northerner. Couldn't figure out why he was wasting his time hanging round with Turanians. Me and Gurd must have saved Thraxas eight or nine times, him being a fat, useless drunk even when he was young.'

We drink a fourth flagon.

'Who was that other Turanian fool you were with?' asks Calbeshi. 'The tall, stupid man with an axe?'

'Poldax. Good man. Survived the war, I remember.'

We get down to swapping war stories. Around us, Calbeshi's men, more industrious than their boss, unload beer and send it off to the Simnian units which now make up the left flank of the army. Droo sits on the wagon, observing everything, looking quite cheerful in her unfamiliar environment. She has a long knife at her hip. I wonder if she can use it in combat. I can't quite imagine Droo going into combat. It might happen sooner than she anticipates. We'll be meeting up with the Niojans any time now. After that, we'll be marching east. We don't have any intelligence about the whereabouts of the Orcish army, but we'll encounter them somewhere.

I drink a few more beers and exchange another round of insults with Calbeshi. Having done my bit for Turanian-Simnian relations, I head off back to my wagon. Droo walks at my side, a little unsteadily. She's quite a small Elf. Doesn't have the capacity of a mighty imbiber like myself. She stumbles. I reach out to steady her. She manages a few more paces then trips over her own feet and sprawls on the ground. Once horizontal, she shows no inclination to rise.

'Damn it, Droo, get up.'

114

'It's comfy here.'

'No doubt. But you have to get up and walk.'

'Why?'

'People are watching. You're destroying the reputation of my Security Unit.'

Droo finds this amusing, and starts to laugh. I'm perplexed, and unsure how to proceed. I can't have members of my unit rolling around drunk on duty. That's a privilege reserved for me. I can hear some sarcastic comments aimed in our direction from a group of Simnian spearmen not far away. Something about the Sorcerers Auxiliary Regiment being full of overweight buffoons and puny Elves. My mood starts to worsen.

'Dammit Droo, will you–'

'Captain Thraxas. I need to talk to you in private.'

It's Captain Hanama. That doesn't improve my mood.

'Can it wait?'

'No. Commander Lisutaris instructs that I inform you of developments.' Hanama looks down at the intoxicated young Elf at her feet. 'I see your security unit is performing as expected.'

I grab Droo by her tunic and haul her upright. She falls down again. I pick her up and throw her over my shoulder. She starts singing an Elvish song, then goes quiet.

'You are aware that drunkenness on duty is against regulations?' says Hanama.

'Just tell me the news, Captain Hanama.'

She casts a disapproving glance at Droo. 'It's confidential.'

'My security unit is completely trustworthy. Anyway, she's sleeping.'

We set off, heading towards my wagon. Captain Hanama lowers her voice as she passes on her news. 'My intelligence unit has uncovered evidence suggesting that the Orcs are attempting to prepare a grand hiding spell, capable of concealing their entire army.'

'That's impossible.'

'So one would have thought. However Lisutaris is taking it seriously. My operative Megleth brought news that the Elvish Ambassador's house in Abelasi was burgled last year. Certain books were stolen from the library. These included an ancient magical tome concerned with hiding an island from the enemy.'

'Hiding an island? That's impossible too.'

'Are you going to continually interrupt by saying everything is impossible? I repeat, Lisutaris is taking this seriously. Intelligence reports also indicate a flow of rare blue quartz crystals from the north to the east over the past year. Someone has been buying them up. These crystals are commonly used in advanced spells of hiding. This, along with certain communications intercepted in the past month, leads me to believe that the Orcish Sorcerers Guild may be attempting to hide their entire army, prior to attack.'

'And our Commander believes this?'

'Yes.'

'Then our Commander isn't thinking clearly. No one can hide an entire army. It's too big and there's too many people. It can't be done. If it could be it would have been done by now.'

Captain Hanama purses her lips. 'I believe you were ejected from sorcerers college after your rudimentary attempts to learn magic came to nothing?'

'You could put it like that.'

'Then you'll forgive me for valuing Lisutaris's opinion over yours. Our Commander is concerned that Deeziz might be able to work such a spell and wanted me to let you know. That I have now done.'

By this time we're close to Lisutaris's command tent. As we approach, we can hear raised voices. Moments later we walk right into the middle of an almighty row. Bishop-General Ritari and Legate Apiroi are engaged in a heated exchange with our War Leader. The Samsarinan General Hemistos and the Elvish Lord Kalith-ar-Yil are standing nearby, looking uncomfortable, as are various other senior officers, including General Mexes and Admiral Arith. Makri is standing close to Lisutaris, glowering at the Niojans.

Legate Apiroi pushes himself forward. 'I insist you tell us the truth about these rumours, Commander. Is there an Orcish sorcerer in our midst?'

'No,' declares Lisutaris. 'And people shouldn't listen to wild rumours.'

'Wild rumours?' cries the Legate. 'More than rumours, I'd say. A sorcerer has been killed, a storm comes out of nowhere, and who knows what else? Are we expected to march under these circumstances? I won't allow the Niojan army to be betrayed before we've even encountered the Orcs.'

At this, Lisutaris looks so furious I'm half-expecting her to blast the Legate with a spell for his insubordination. She restrains herself, probably because Bishop-General Ritari is at his side. As head of the Niojan contingent, Ritari can't be blasted with a spell. Not unless we want the army to fall apart.

Lisutaris looks Legate Apiroi in the eye. 'I am War Leader,' she says. 'And I don't answer to you.'

'But I answer to King Lamachus of Nioj.'

I take a step forward. I feel a small tugging at my sleeve.

'Don't start abusing everyone,' whispers Droo. 'It won't help.'

I suppose she's right. I take a step back, though I don't like the way this is shaping up. In the interests of cohesion and co-operation, Lisutaris has purposely given out senior posts to her allies, rather than fellow Turanians, but if things go wrong, it could leave her isolated. She's looking isolated at the moment. Captain Julius, her aide-de-camp, isn't the sort of forceful personality who can fend off irate generals.

'King Lamachus supports me as War Leader.'

'Provisionally supports you,' says Legate Apiroi. 'Depending on my official reports.'

This is an outrageous piece of effrontery, even by the Legate's standards. General Hemistos and Lord Kalith-ar-Yil both look towards Lisutaris, wondering how she's going to react. The Legate's intransigence is putting her in a difficult position. She can't let herself be seen to be back down, but neither can she do anything which might give the Niojans an excuse to withdraw. I step forward. Droo tugs at my sleeve again. 'Don't worry,' I mutter. 'I'll be tactful.'

'Legate Apiroi,' I say, loud enough for everyone to hear. 'There are no Orcish sorcerers within fifty miles of us. But if you're terrified by a few wild rumours, maybe you should scuttle back to Nioj, while real warriors like myself and Commander Lisutaris go and chase the Orcs back east. No one will miss you.'

Droo laughs. Makri almost smiles. For the rest, there's a frozen silence, soon broken by the outraged protests of Legate Apiroi, Bishop-General Ritari, and the various junior Niojan officers behind them. The perimeter guards edge forward, wondering if they're going to have to prevent a fight breaking out among the ranks of their commanders. That would be unusual, though not unheard of. The scene quickly degenerates, with the Niojan high-command yelling at me and me yelling at them, while General Hemistos and the Elvish Lord seek some clarification from Lisutaris about what's been going on. It's an ugly scene, but you might say it's better than having Lisutaris face a barrage of questions and accusations to which she has no easy answer.

Lisutaris raises her hand and yells for silence. The shouting dies down.

'Bishop-General,' she says, ignoring the Legate. 'Is the Cavalry ready to advance?'

'Yes, but–'

'Then return to them and prepare to advance.' Lisutaris turns to General Hemistos. 'The infantry?'

'All units ready, Commander.'

'Good. Make ready to advance, Lord Kalith, return to your Elvish units and prepare to move forward. Everyone return to your units. It's time to move. Senior officers will convene for our normal meeting in the evening.'

The War Leader glares at them all, daring any of them to defy her. Hemistos nods briefly then hurries off, pleased to be away from the argument. Lord Kalith-ar-Yil hesitates for a few seconds, before he too departs. The Niojans are still reluctant. Bishop-General Ritari stares at Lisutaris, clearly dissatisfied, before finally turning to leave, taking the Legate with him. I watch them go.

'Legate Apiroi certainly thinks well of himself. I'd say Bishop-General Ritari should watch his back.'

'Captain Thraxas,' says Lisutaris. 'Why are you carrying Ensign Sendroo?'

That's a difficult question to answer.

'Has she been drinking?'

Again that's not a question I'm keen to answer.

'Captain Thraxas, in my tent, now. Captain Hanama, you also. Captain Julius, send for sorcerer Irith Victorious. I want him here immediately.'

Captain Julius hurries off. I place Ensign Sendroo on the ground then follow warily behind Lisutaris into the command tent. I have the vague feeling that she's not very pleased with me.

Chapter Fifteen

For once I don't mind that Hanama is around. It might not be the best time to be alone with our War Leader. She appears to be in a very poor temper. Understandable, after the confrontation with the Niojans, though there's no reason take it out on me. It's not my fault.

'Captain Thraxas,' roars Lisutaris. 'I regard this as mainly your fault!'

'My fault?'

'Yes, your fault. How do you think Legate Apiroi learned of Deeziz? She obviously tipped him off somehow. Probably with an anonymous message. That woman is causing chaos in my camp and now she's letting my enemies know about it!'

'I suppose that's quite likely–'

'And who's responsibility was it to prevent that happening? Yours! If you'd spent as much time looking for Deeziz as you have swilling ale with the Simnian Quartermaster, perhaps you'd have found her by now.'

'Swilling ale? Has Anumaris been spying on me again? She really exaggerates–'

'Exaggerates? One of your security unit is sprawled on the ground outside this tent, incapacitated after another of your endless binges! No wonder you can't find Deeziz. She could walk by in her best Orcish sorcerer's costume and you probably wouldn't even notice. When I appointed you as my personal head of security I expected you to do some security! So far your futile efforts have come to nothing, and it's not good enough!'

Lisutaris turns towards Hanama. She's a tall woman, and towers over the diminutive assassin. 'As for you, Captain Hanama, you've fared no better. Your intelligence unit has brought me no useful information regarding Deeziz and your much-vaunted Elvish agent is a complete waste of time.' Lisutaris picks up a sheet of parchment from her desk and glares at it. 'Field report from Megleth. Have found no trace of Prince Amrag's army. Suspect they may be hidden by superior sorcery.'

Lisutaris flings the report back on the desk. 'What use it that? We can't find Amrag's army? I knew that already! When you persuaded me to employ that damned Elvish assassin you claimed she was the finest spy in the business.'

'She is extremely talented, Commander,' says Hanama, who, I'm pleased to note, is looking uncomfortable under criticism. She deserves it.

'Extremely talented? If she had any talent she'd have found the Orcish army! How hard can that be? It's not like it's easy to hide! It's an army! With thousands of Orcs! But your best agent can't find it?'

'Perhaps she's right about the superior sorcery,' mutters Hanama.

'You told me Megleth the Elf could not be baffled by sorcery!'

'Usually she can't be,' mutters Hanama, hopelessly. 'Perhaps it's the grand hiding spell...'

'The grand hiding spell!' cries Lisutaris. 'Another useless piece of information. So far all you've learned is that the Orcs have been hoarding crystals and stealing books. Can Deeziz perform the spell or not? Can she hide their army?'

'I don't know.'

'Then find out! Stop sending me useless reports and actually do something about it!'

Hanama looks at Lisutaris hopelessly, stuck for an answer. While I'm enjoying seeing the assassin criticised, I suspect that Lisutaris will be returning to me soon enough. It's therefore a relief when Irith Victorious hurries into the tent. Not that much of a relief, admittedly. Irith Victorious detests me for robbing and betraying him at the Sorcerers Assemblage. My explanation that it was necessary for the glory of Turai didn't do anything to make things better.

'There you are, Irith,' says Lisutaris. 'Everything fine with you and your sorcerers' detection unit?'

'Yes, Commander.'

'I'm pleased to hear it. Remember that small task I gave you?'

It's Irith's turn to look uncomfortable. He's a large man, almost as large as me. At the Assemblage there was no one jollier, and no one drank more either. He's not looking that jolly at the moment.

'Well?'

'No progress, Commander,' admits Irith.

'Why would I expect anything else? I ask you and your supposedly high-powered Abelasian sorcerers to find Deeziz the Unseen and have you done it? Of course not. You're just as useless as Thraxas and Hanama.'

'We're trying our best,' protests Irith.

'Your best? Really? Is that what you call it? You have access to every piece of investigating sorcery known in the west, plus my own memories of Deeziz. That should be more than enough to detect her. So why haven't you?'

'There's something wrong,' says Irith, hopelessly.

'Something wrong?' Lisutaris positively erupts with rage. 'That's a fantastic insight, Irith! Of course there's something wrong! You can't find an enemy sorcerer who's right in our midst!'

'If she was using any normal hiding spells we'd have broken through by now. I think she must be using some sort of magic we haven't encountered before.'

At this our War Leader almost explodes. She castigates the unfortunate Irith Victorious and his fellow Abelasians. 'Don't ever come in here again and tell me Deeziz is using magic you haven't encountered before!' she cries. 'That's been obvious from the start, you hopeless excuse for a sorcerer! Your task is to discover it and counter it! Can you grasp that simple fact?'

'Yes, Commander,' mumbles Irith.

Lisutaris sweeps an angry gaze around all of us. 'As my heads of security, intelligence, and sorcerous enquiry, you're all a complete washout. You, Thraxas, are about as much use as a one-legged gladiator. I can't believe I ever put my faith in you. Irith Victorious, my grandmother had more sorcerous power than you, and she only used her spells for cooking. And you, Captain Hanama, would be well advised to stop sneaking round the camp pretending to gather intelligence and actually do something useful, like help find Deeziz. Or else you could actually locate the Orcish army. Unless you'd rather just let them waltz up without warning and slaughter us all while we sleep?'

No one replies. There doesn't seem to be anything to say. During all this, Makri has been hovering in the background, looking smug. It's a nasty surprise for her when Lisutaris rounds on her too.

'I don't see why you're looking so pleased with yourself. You didn't do such a great job when we visited the Oracle, did you? If you had, then perhaps Ibella Hailstorm wouldn't be dead. And maybe if you spent less time ogling young Elves you'd be able to concentrate more on your duties. Unless you'd rather just drink with Thraxas of course. Perhaps he could find you some dwa. Why don't you all just join him in his wagon for a pleasant little party while I try and lead this army at the same time as the Head of The Orcish Sorcerers Guild is making a complete fool of me?'

Makri is rendered speechless. There's a very uncomfortable pause before Lisutaris orders us out of her command tent. When we troop outside, the guards, who've probably heard every word, sneer at us as we pass. Droo clambers to her feet and follows us as we depart.

'I don't think that was justified,' says Makri, in a subdued tone. 'I haven't been ogling young Elves. I might have glanced in their direction when they were swimming in the river. There was really nothing to it.'

No one else speaks. There's not much to say. We go our separate ways. I can't believe our War Leader accused me of being as useless as a one-legged gladiator. It's hardly the sort of language you expect from the aristocratic Head of the Sorcerers Guild. I'm thoughtful as I walk back to my wagon, and depressingly sober. Simnian beer, it's just not that good. Wears off far too quickly.

Anumaris Thunderbolt is sitting with the reins in her hands, trundling forward slowly as the army gets underway again. She greets me quite formally. I doubt she admires Captain Thraxas any more than Lisutaris does. I decide to lie down for a while. Perhaps I'll feel inspired after I've slept. Before I nod off, a thought strikes me. I try and ignore it. The thought won't go away. I curse, and sit up. I'm remembering the time I was down in Mattesh with Gurd.

That useless Simnian Calbeshi was there too, stealing a living by pretending to be a mercenary. Must have been twenty years ago. More, perhaps. There was another Turanian with us. Poldax. A large man with an axe. I hadn't thought about him for years till Calbeshi reminded me of him. I don't know what happened to him after that campaign. Something's nagging at me. What is it? I shake my head and look around for some beer. There isn't any. Damn this war.

Another name floats into my head. Poldius. Lisutaris said that Tirini's father was called Poldius. A respectable palace official. I've lived all my life in Turai and I've never heard that family name. I drag myself upright and poke my head through the flap at the front of the wagon to talk to Anumaris. Her long sorcerers cloak is covered in dust, as is the scarf tied round her face.

'Have you ever heard of a Turanian called Poldius?'

She lowers the scarf to speak. 'I don't think so.'

'Are you sure? He'd be one of your class.'

Anumaris is sure she's never heard of him.

'Do you have any idea where Dasinius might be? The palace scribe who was looking after Turanian refugees when they arrived in Samsarina. Did he travel with the army?'

'If he did, he'd be with the other non-combatant Turanian officials in the administrative division. Their wagons are about a hundred metres behind us, a little to the right.'

I drop off our wagon, make my way to the clear pathway that's maintained between traffic at all times, and wait for the army to slowly pass. When I spot a group of wagons with a Turanian flag fluttering above them and some elderly faces among the passengers, I cross over to them and ask for Dasinius. I'm directed to one of the Turanian vehicles where I find the palace scribe on the pillion, with the reins in his hands. Like Anumaris, he has a scarf tied round the lower part of his face, protecting him from the dust kicked up by the advancing army. He looks at me sourly.

'What do you want?'

'A brief talk about the population of Turai.'

I climb up beside him, to his obvious displeasure. None of the Officials I know from my time working at the Palace seem to remember me fondly. Class prejudice, I'd say.

'You used to work at the Palace Registry, didn't you? Recording births and deaths, and marriages and so on?'

'I was head of the department.' He sounds proud of it. I never thought it was that important a position.

'Did you ever come across anyone called Poldius?'

'No.'

'Are you sure?'

'Yes I'm sure. There was no Poldius in Turai.'

'Maybe you just never met him?'

Dasinius lowers his scarf and casts a baleful look in my direction. 'It's bad enough being chased out of Turai at my age, without having to answer questions from you, Thraxas, one-time investigator at the Palace. What did they kick you out for? Drunkenness? Laziness? Or were you cheating on your expenses?'

'Just answer the question, Dasinius. I'm personal security officer for Lisutaris. You don't want to annoy her.'

The elderly official laughs. 'Annoy Lisutaris? I don't give a damn. My life's going to end fighting Orcs who've captured my city and outsmarted us at every turn. Lisutaris isn't going to make any difference.'

Apparently Turanian morale is not as high as might be.

'About Poldius...?'

'There's no Poldius. I'd recognise the family name.'

'No Poldius in all of Turai? Ever?'

'Damn you Thraxas, how many times do I have to tell you?'

I mull this over for a minute or two. Dasinius coughs, and pulls the scarf back over his mouth.

'What about Poldax?'

'What about him?'

'He was a little older than me. Fought as a mercenary down in Mattesh.'

'I know, I remember him. I filed his marriage certificate. And his death certificate, about fifteen years ago.'

'What did he do?'

125

'He was a municipal worker. Employed by the Ministry of Civil Works to inspect the sewers.'

'Did he have any children?'

Dasinius thinks for a few moments. 'One daughter. Tirina.'

He does have an impressive knowledge of the city-state's inhabitants. I wonder if he can remember every single one.

'Tirina? What happened to her?'

Dasinius shrugs. 'I don't know. I don't recall ever filing a certificate for her - not for marriage, or death, or anything else. Maybe she left the city.'

I thank Dasinius. After leaving him I walk quickly up the line, passing the slow-moving wagons till I catch up with my own. Anumaris is still driving, Droo is still sleeping. I'm due for some sleep myself. I use my cloak as a pillow and lie down. I have a few more things to think about now. I need my rest.

Chapter Sixteen

The next day, rumours sweep through the army. Deeziz the Unseen's name is suddenly on everyone's lips. Everyone seems to know that the most powerful Orcish sorcerer is here, right in the middle of our army, undetected. The mood among the soldiers changes from optimism to apprehension. The storm which delayed us, previously seen as an unfortunate natural phenomenon, is now taken as proof of Deeziz's power. It's a severe blow to morale. Even though our rendezvous with the Niojans has been delayed, the army was in good spirits. Not any more. The shocking rumours have a devastating effect. Everywhere you look there are soldiers eying their neighbours suspiciously, wondering if they might be an Orcish spy or an Orcish sorcerer. Confidence in Lisutaris as War Leader has plummeted.

I'm sitting morosely in the back of my wagon when Droo clambers in with a half-full bottle of wine in her hand. It's an inferior vintage but that can't be helped. If it wasn't for Droo's excellent talent for sniffing out spare supplies of alcohol, I'd have been in a much worse state.

'Deeziz is a cunning Orc,' I mutter, after a hefty swig from the wine bottle. 'She's spreading rumours about her own presence. Now the troops are worried and Lisutaris looks bad.'

It could get worse. If Deeziz decides to transmit some anonymous messages to the Niojans about Lisutaris visiting the oracle, it might end our alliance.

Rinderan appears. The young sorcerer is carrying a list of names. 'Sorcerer Irith and his companions have checked every name on this list,' he informs me. 'They've come up with nothing.'

'Did they really look?'

'So Irith says. They've used all available sorcery and examined everyone close to our War Leader. Every Commander, every one of her personal staff, anyone who's been in contact with her. They've also checked everyone in the army who has any sorcerous power - the front line combat sorcerers, the message senders, the medical sorcerers, even the weather unit. No one shows any sign of actually being an Orcish imposter.'

I grunt with exasperation. According to Irith, his sorcerous detection unit had developed some new tools of magical investigation which he regarded as foolproof. Obviously they weren't. I take the list and dismiss Rinderan, rather wearily. The whole affair is starting to seem hopeless. The list contains details of every possible suspect, anyone close enough to Lisutaris to know details of her plans. It's a depressingly long. There's her war council - General Hemistos, Lord Kalith-ar-Yil, and Bishop-General Ritari. Her aide-de-camp Julius. My own security staff. Makri. Irith Victorious and his fellow Abelasian sorcerers. Captain Hanama and her staff, including the mysterious Megleth, Elvish assassin. Then there's Tirini, and her nursemaid Saabril Eclipse. The two Kamaran sorcerers they arrived with. Coranius the Grinder. There are the trusted guards who are always in place around her command tent. They're not senior officers but they're in close enough proximity to Lisutaris to learn a lot of information if they wanted. Senior Storm Class Sorcerer Habintenat and his weather unit. The officers in the level below the command council, General Mexes and Admiral Arith. All of these people have already been examined, both by my own unit and Irith's sorcerers. I stare at the list, vaguely hoping that some inspiration might strike. A half hour later, I'm still staring when Makri climbs into the wagon. Her hair is pulled back tightly and tied in a long pony-tail, perhaps as part of an effort to look more disciplined. I ask her if she's hiding from See-ath.

'No. He hasn't been around. Lisutaris asked me to leave for a while.'

'Another top-secret commanders' meeting?'

Makri frowns. 'She says she's meeting Legate Apiroi. I don't like it.'

'Why would she meet him?'

'I don't know. Yesterday she wanted him kept out the way and today they're having a private conference. It can't mean anything good. Legate Apiroi is only interested in one thing, increasing his influence. I think he's trying to usurp Bishop-General Ritari. Wouldn't surprise me if he's got ambitions to be War Leader.'

Makri takes the bottle of wine from me and drinks. 'I don't like it. Lisutaris should just get rid of him.'

'She has to be tactful. Relations with Nioj are always tricky.'

Makri notices the scroll in my hand. 'What are you reading?'

'My list of every possible suspect.'

'Is it helping?'

'No, it's useless. There must be forty or fifty people who've had enough contact with Lisutaris to be doing this damage. My unit has run background checks on all of them. Irith Victorious has checked them with sorcery. No results. If Deeziz is so clever maybe it doesn't matter what sort of checks we make. Perhaps she can just fake anything. Maybe she can plant false memories in people.'

'Is that possible?'

'I don't know. I'm beginning to wonder if there's anything this Orc can't do. She must have done a lot of studying on that mountain top. Maybe Lisutaris did go to too many parties.'

I take another sip from the wine bottle. 'I always knew our degenerate aristocracy would ruin Turai. Lisutaris and Tirini spend their whole time dancing and gossiping at Palace soirées while Deeziz does what a sorcerer is meant to do - learn more sorcery. And now look what's happened. Tirini's half-dead, Lisutaris has gone mad, and an honest man like myself has his name dragged through the mud by malicious prophesies from a corrupt High Priestess. I tell you Makri, the situation is bad. We can't even find the Orcish army. So much for Hanama and her Intelligence Unit. We've got a Sorcerous Weather Unit that can't stop storms, and a Sorcerous Investigation Unit that couldn't find an Orc if she walked up and introduced herself.'

'In other words, everyone else is to blame?' says Makri.

'Exactly. Useless, degenerate incompetents, all of them.'

'How much wine have you drunk?'

'Not enough. I can't believe Lisutaris said I was as much use as a one-legged gladiator. That's not the sort of crude expression you expect to hear from your War Leader.'

'I didn't like being blamed for Ibella's death. But Lisutaris is under a lot of pressure. She's worried she's not going to be able to hold the army together.'

'All the more reason to value her trusted companions. I rescued that woman from Turai!'

'Are you ever going to stop bragging about that?' Makri drinks from the bottle.

'I blame the oracle.'

'The oracle?'

'We've been cursed since we visited that place. I hate oracles. They're always useless. Some mumbo-jumbo that no one can understand. You never find an oracle saying anything worthwhile like "Tomorrow someone will buy you a flagon of ale and a mutton pie." That would be an oracle worth having.'

'It's interesting how powerful a grip oracles still have on people's imaginations,' says Makri.

'People are fools. Oracles are nonsense.'

Makri shrugs. 'I know. Though it's odd how accurate some of the High Priestess's predictions were. Ibella died of poison right after she was warned to fear only poison.'

'That's only one prophesy. Anyone can get lucky. I still think her words to Hanama were ridiculous. *Much Death.* Hanama's an assassin, it didn't take tremendous insight to come up with that.'

'Did the High Priestess know she was an assassin?'

'Probably. It wouldn't surprise me if her followers sneaked her some hints about the people who visit her. Charlatans, all of them. As for Gurd, and *Much Life*–' I pause. 'Now I think about it, Gurd told me Tanrose wants to have a baby. I suppose that might qualify as much life.'

Makri is amused. 'Maybe the High Priestess knew what she was talking about.'

I refuse to rise to the bait. I know Makri has no more belief in oracles than me.

'Why did Gurd tell you Tanrose wanted to have a baby?'

'Because he knows I'm one of the few sensible men left in the west, and he wanted advice.'

'What did you tell him?'

'Mainly that I didn't want to talk about babies.'

'He'd be a good father,' says Makri.

'He would be. But he's worried he won't be alive long enough to see the child. That's a sensible worry. If this campaign continues to go downhill none of us will be around for long.'

We're still trundling slowly over the low hills on the approach to the border between Simnia and Nioj. We'll be meeting up with the Niojan army any time now. I wonder what sort of reports Legate Apiroi and Bishop-General Ritari have been sending them.

'I found out something odd about Tirini Snake Smiter,' I tell Makri, lowering my voice so that Anumaris won't overhear. 'She doesn't come from the respectable family she claims. I don't think she came from Turai's upper class at all. Her father was a sewer inspector. If he's the man I used to know, he was about as low class as me, which is very low, in Turanian terms.'

'Why would Tirini lie about that?'

'You lived in Turai long enough to know what it's like. Class makes a lot of difference. The upper classes are obsessed with status and they don't like sharing their privileges.'

Makri, as a foreign female gladiator with Orcish blood, had the lowest status it was possible to have in Turai, so she knows what I'm talking about. Even so, she's puzzled about Tirini.

'Sorcerers don't have to come from the aristocracy, do they?'

'Most sorcerers are the sons and daughters of respectable families. Not the highest aristocracy, but respectable. There are a few from the lower classes but they don't get far in the Sorcerers Guild. Not promoted to the best posts. I suppose Tirini didn't want to admit her background, particularly as she was so obsessed with being Turai's most glamorous woman. I can understand that. But I'm puzzled.'

'Why?'

'I wouldn't have thought it would have been easy for her to hide her background from other sorcerers. Not when she started out, anyway. When she first went to the Sorcerers College, she couldn't have had that much power. The professors there should have seen through any attempt at deception. They do look into their students' backgrounds as part of the induction process.'

Makri takes a small bag from a pocket inside her armoured tunic.

'Lisutaris gave me this.'

'So she hasn't stopped using it?'

'She's cut down a lot. Quite a lot. Well, she doesn't smoke as much as she used to.'

Makri rolls up the thazis into a stick and lights it. She inhales then passes it to me. We smoke it peacefully together for a few minutes.

'What's wrong with being a sewer inspector anyway?' asks Makri.

'Pardon?'

'You said Tirini was ashamed of her father being a sewer inspector. I don't see why anyone would be ashamed of working on the sewers. Haven't you used them during your investigations?'

'Once or twice.'

'And we escaped from the city via the sewers. You might say they saved Lisutaris's life. Anyway, they're a good piece of architecture.'

'They are?'

'Of course. Turai's sewerage system is one of the best there is, in any city. It was all designed by the Master Architect Janavius.'

'How do you know that?'

'I learned in college. If it wasn't for the innovations made by Janavius, Turai would be the festering mess it deserves to be. He built eight new tunnels under the city, incorporating three ancient streams into the system, and he was responsible for–'

I hold up my hand. 'Makri, does it ever worry you that you seem able to deliver a lecture on any conceivable subject?'

'No.'

'It worries me.'

'I think you just resent that women can get a good education at the Guild College.'

'I only resent it when they're lecturing me about it.' I inhale from the thazis stick and pass it back to Makri. 'I'll take your word that our sewers are a marvel of architecture. It might take a while to convince the rest of the population. I can see why Tirini tried to keep it quiet.'

'I suppose so. Though Janavius really deserves more credit for his work. Did you know he was responsible for adding volcanic ash to concrete, which means it can set underwater? He discovered this by–'

I sigh, and try to block of Makri's lecture on Turai's marvel of underground architecture. Once she gets going on this sort of thing, she can be hard to stop. It's almost a relief when Anumaris Thunderbolt pokes her head through the canvas flap with an angry expression on her face.

'I thought I smelled thazis! You shouldn't be smoking that.'

'Why not?'

'You shouldn't be intoxicated when you're on duty.'

'We're off duty.'

'No you are not. What if some crisis happens?'

'Then you can deal with it.'

I pass the thazis stick back to Makri. 'I thought you were bad, lecturing me about drinking all the time. Anumaris here is ten times worse.'

'I'm just doing my duty!' protests the young sorcerer. 'We're on our way to war. We should be alert at all times. Something could happen.'

'Just drive the wagon, Anumaris. Nothing is going to happen.'

At that moment, Lisutaris, War Leader, Commander of the Western Armies, appears at the rear of the wagon. She climbs in, quite nimbly.

'I told you something might happen,' says Anumaris.

Chapter Seventeen

I notice our Commander glancing at the thazis stick in Makri's hand and the bottle of wine in mine. 'We were just discussing my investigation.'

Lisutaris scowls. 'Have you ever gone through a day without a bottle or flagon in your hand?'

'Eight days at sea, without beer, in a leaky boat, Commander. After I rescued you from Turai.'

Lisutaris smiles, which is a surprise, given her recent hostility. 'I should probably be grateful it's your only vice,' she says. She reaches into her purse and pulls out a bag of thazis, rolling herself a stick with dexterity born of long practice.

'I don't think you can say that drinking is Thraxas's only vice,' says Makri. 'You'd have to mention gluttony as well. And gambling. He really has a problem with gambling.'

'I've come to talk to you about something important—' begins Lisutaris.

'Then there's the bad language. And what about his laziness? Sometimes you just can't move him, no matter what.'

'You forgot my tendency to violence,' I growl.

'You see? Drinking, gambling, violence, It's just one thing after another. I don't see how you can say that drinking is Thraxas's only vice. It's just not an accurate description of the man.'

Lisutaris purses her lips. 'I believe you've made your point, Ensign Makri. If I might be allowed to speak?'

'Of course, Commander.'

Lisutaris nudges Droo awake with her toe. 'Junior Ensign Sendroo, go outside, get Anumaris, and make sure no one listens to my conversation in here.'

The young Elf nods, and departs swiftly. Lisutaris waves her hand briefly and mutters a spell.

'What was that?'

'To prevent anyone listening in. We can't be too careful.' The Sorceress inhales deeply from her thazis stick. 'I've just been in discussion with Legate Apiroi. I'd rather not have been but he sent me a message I couldn't ignore. Apparently the Legate has learned I went to the oracle.'

'How?'

'He wouldn't say. I presume Deeziz was behind it. She seems to have a talent for sending anonymous messages and sowing discord. Apiroi thinks he has me in a tough spot. He's threatened to tell King Lamachus about my visit unless I promote him to my command council.'

'That's outrageous!' cries Makri. 'He can't blackmail you! You're War Leader.'

'Apiroi seems capable of anything. He's one of the most ambitious reptiles I've ever encountered. He's determined to take over as leader of the Niojan faction, and if he's after my position as well, I wouldn't be surprised.'

Lisutaris pauses to inhale from her thazis stick. 'All in all, it was a difficult meeting.'

'What are you going to do?' asks Makri.

'I told him I'd consider his proposal.'

'How long will that hold him off for?'

'Long enough for me to deal with the situation.'

'How are you planning to deal with it?' I enquire.

Lisutaris exhales a stream of thazis smoke. 'That's not something I can tell you. But I will deal with it.'

I notice that the sorceress seems relatively composed, given the possible gravity of her position. I wonder what she means when she says she'll deal with it.

'However that's not really why I'm here,' says Lisutaris. 'I've come to tell you that I have to leave camp again, in secret. Tonight.'

'The Niojans are arriving tonight.'

Lisutaris nods. 'That makes it awkward. I should be here to greet their leaders. Nonetheless, I have to make an excursion.'

'Why?'

'The High Priestess of Vitina is bringing me my Oracle.'

'What?' I almost explode. 'That's insane. You've just told us that Legate Apiroi is trying to blackmail you about your last visit. Now you want to see the High Priestess again?'

'It is unfortunate timing. That's why I'm keeping it secret. No one will know apart from you and Makri. Neither of you are Deeziz. After eight days on a boat together, I know you too well. I never thought I'd be grateful for that.'

Makri is agitated. 'Lisutaris,' she begins, forgetting to call her Commander, as she normally would. 'I don't think this is a good idea. It's far too dangerous. Last time Deeziz ambushed us. It could happen again.'

'What if we run into the whole Orcish Army? We don't even know where they are.'

'The fact that we can't locate the Orcish army is a good reason for going. I'm hoping the High Priestess might have some news for me. She sent me a message that my Oracle is ready, and I need to have it.'

I remain firmly against the idea. 'Can't she come here and give you it in person?'

'The High Priestess would not come near the Niojans, who outlawed her religion. Or any of the True Church officials who travel with the army.'

'Well I'd hate to inconvenience her. But I think she might make the effort. Couldn't she send a letter?'

'No. The oracle must be delivered in person, in an appropriate place. I'm going to meet her in a small temple of the Goddess Vitina, not far from here. It's deserted these days, but still suitable for the transmission of a prophesy. It's quite an honour. The High Priestess does not normally make journeys.'

I put the wine bottle to my mouth. It's empty. Makri passes me her thazis stick. 'Commander, this is a really bad idea. As your Personal Security Officer, I advise against it. We fought the Orcs together fifteen years ago. We were on the same wall in Turai when it collapsed. I know what I'm talking about when it comes to Orcs, and security. Don't leave the army and wander off on your own.'

Lisutaris is inhaling from another thazis stick. The wagon is thick with pungent smoke.

'Sorry, Thraxas,' she says. 'I do value your opinion. But we're going.'

'If Legate Apiroi does tell people that you visited the oracle, and then you do it again, the Niojans won't follow you as War Leader,' says Makri.

'I know. But I need the High Priestess's prophesy. The Goddess Vitina is more important to me than the Niojans.'

'Is it reasonable to expect me to meet that High Priestess again? Last time she told me I'd throw down my shield and flee. I'm still insulted.'

Lisutaris shrugs. 'Maybe your prophesy will work out well?'

'How can throwing down my shield and fleeing work out well?'

'No matter. We're going. The three of us. Tonight. Don't mention it to anyone else. I'll make sure we leave the camp unseen.'

I'm dead set against it, but there's nothing to be done. Lisutaris, Mistress of the Sky, War Leader, Commander, and Head of the Western Sorcerers Guild, has made up her mind to ride off into the wilds and meet this fraudulent High Priestess.

'I anticipate disaster,' I mutter.

Lisutaris reaches into her bag. It's a small, stylish bag, but it contains a magic pocket, which can carry anything. She brings out a bottle of beer.

'I brought you this.'

I take the beer and open the bottle. 'This isn't enough to make up for it.'

'It's all you're going to get.' She inhales from her thazis, and sits back against the side of the wagon. 'Not such a bad wagon you have here. It's peaceful after my command tent. I'm already fatigued with generals, diplomats and senior sorcerers.'

Lisutaris's spell for ensuring that we're not overheard seems to block off all sound from the outside. We sit in silence for a few minutes, drinking beer and smoking thazis. Lisutaris relaxes a little. She looks up at Makri.

'That idiot Kublinos has been parading round my command tent with his Elvish sorceress again. Or so-called sorceress. From what I hear, she doesn't have much power. Do you think she's attractive?'

'No,' says Makri, showing more tact than normal. Lisutaris turns to me. 'Do you think she's attractive?'

'I haven't seen her.'

'You must have. Kublinos is always walking round with her like she's some great catch. You'd think he was the only human sorcerer ever to attract an Elf. With fading looks. And virtually no power. I doubt she even belongs in the Sorcerers Guild. Probably she only was admitted due to family influence. What he sees in her, I have no idea. She has peculiar eyes. Did you notice how strange her eyes are?'

'Really strange,' says Makri.

'I don't see how you can have missed her, Thraxas. Just look for the female Elvish sorcerer with funny eyes, no magical power, and very poor dress sense. You'd recognise her right away. She's always trailing round after Kublinos. I almost feel sorry for him.'

'I thought you didn't care about Kublinos?'

Lisutaris's eyes flash. 'Of course I don't care about Kublinos! What makes you think I do?'

'The way you keep talking about him and his new lady friend?'

'Absolute nonsense. Makri, has anything I've said given you the remotest impression that I'm at all bothered about Kublinos?'

'No, Commander.' Makri, who has never shown the slightest tact in regards to me, has obviously learned how to use some discretion around our War Leader.

'The fact is,' continues Lisutaris. 'Kublinos is obviously obsessed with me. He never stops parading around with that woman in tow, as if it's going to upset me. It's childish behaviour. I'm astonished at his immaturity.' She rises to her feet. 'Meet me in my tent at two in the morning. Don't mention it to anyone else and don't be late.'

With that, she departs. I look over at Makri. 'Does this Elvish sorcerer really have funny eyes and poor dress sense?'

'No, she's gorgeous,' says Makri. 'But I wouldn't advise saying that to Lisutaris.'

I sigh. 'You see, this is why women shouldn't go to war. Now we're all going to die because Lisutaris is distracted by some man she claimed not to care for in the first place. As far as I can see, there's only one female sorcerer who's any good at sorcery, and she's on the other side. I'll wager Deeziz the Unseen isn't wasting her time complaining about some petty romantic disappointment.'

I'm not looking forward to tonight's excursion. Damn that High Priestess. She could hardly be putting us in more danger if she was working for the enemy. Maybe she is working for the enemy. Oracles have been known to succumb to bribery. I gaze at my empty beer bottle. I have a feeling of impending doom, and one bottle of beer isn't enough to shift it.

Chapter Eighteen

Makri and I slip out of the wagon one hour after midnight. Anumaris and Droo know we're going somewhere but I've ordered them to keep their mouths shut and not ask questions. Anumaris isn't happy about it. She regards us suspiciously as we leave, probably imagining we're on our way to an all-night drinking session. I wish we were.

Earlier in the evening there were two bright moons in the sky, and the third was dim on the horizon. Now a chilling wind has brought over thick cloud cover and we have to pick our way carefully through the darkened military camp. The guards outside Lisutaris's tent wave us through. The Head of the Sorcerers Guild is waiting for us. There's a short sword on her hip. I haven't often seen Lisutaris wear a sword, though I do remember her hewing at an Orc on the walls of Turai, when she'd expended all her sorcery. She doesn't respond to our greeting. Instead, she holds up her magic purse, and mutters a word. The mouth of the purse grows until it's large enough to step inside. I'm not eager to take the necessary step.

'We're travelling through the magic space?'

'It will get us out of the camp unobserved.'

'It's dangerous to travel that far in the magic space. It almost killed Tirini.'

'She travelled too quickly,' says Lisutaris. 'I'll be more careful.'

Makri is no more enthusiastic than I as we follow Lisutaris into the enlarged mouth of her purse. She's been in the magic space, and it's never enjoyable. Many strange things happen there, and you can never predict what's coming next. It's hazardous, even if you enter and leave at the same location. Lisutaris plans to move us some distance through the real world, which is particularly dangerous. Tirini Snake Smiter is still gravely ill.

I'm thinking about Tirini as I step into the magic space. Something is prodding at my mind. What is it? I've no time to dwell on it as I'm buffeted by freezing winds and a flurry of snow. Bad weather in the magic space; another common problem. We're walking on ice. I pull my cloak around me, shivering as I traipse after Lisutaris and Makri. The sorceress leads us over the ice for a few hundred yards, then halts. She points to a frozen mountain-top in the distance, then mutters a few words, quite softly. Immediately we find ourselves on the mountain.

'No problems so far,' says Lisutaris. At that moment a gigantic eagle swoops from the sky and attempts to bite her head off. Lisutaris is taken by surprise but Makri leaps to her rescue, drawing her sword and decapitating the eagle in one swift movement. Lisutaris looks at the bloody remains at her feet.

'No problems apart from a hostile giant eagle. Let's go.'

We follow her along a treacherous path round the summit of the mountain. It's freezing cold, the snow is eighteen inches deep and my feet are turning to blocks of ice. I'm wearing a good pair of army boots but they weren't designed for mountaineering in winter. It's oddly quiet, the only sound being our footsteps, crunching our way through the snow I've thrust my hands deep in my pockets though Makri keeps her sword drawn and studies our surroundings carefully as we advance.

'Looks like a place where there might be ice mountain trolls,' she says.

'There's no such thing.'

'Yes there is.'

At that moment three huge ice mountain trolls appear from nowhere, each seven foot tall, and each of them carrying a huge wooden club.

'Dammit Makri! You had to go on about ice-mountain trolls!' I draw my sword. The trolls charge towards us. Lisutaris extends both hands and fires off a bolt of blue light that fans out, engulfing all three trolls, sending them spinning off down the mountain side.

'Come on,' she says.

We follow her.

'Don't mention anything else bad,' I tell Makri.

'I didn't make the trolls appear.'

'Then it was an odd co-incidence. This is the magic space, you never know what might happen.'

'Remember we met a talking pig?' Maki smiles, remembering a previous visit we made to the magic space. I don't share her amusement. The talking pig wasn't so bad, I admit, but plenty of other bad things happened. The sky abruptly changes colour, turning a flaming orange followed by a deep red. The snow melts away as warm rain begins to fall. The ground beneath our feet suddenly turns lush and green, and grass sprouts around our ankles, then over our knees, making progress difficult. We struggle on. Makri uses her blade to scythe away the grass which is now growing to waist height. A tree erupts in front of her.

'Foul Orc!' cries the tree. 'Defiling this land!'

Makri looks offended. I almost laugh, till the tree calls me fat.

'I don't know why vegetation in the magic space is always so hostile,' I mutter, batting away a bush that tries to nibble at my ankle. 'What did we ever do to it?'

The grass, bushes and trees grow and merge till we find ourselves in the middle of a dense jungle. It's almost impossible to move.

'Not much further,' says Lisutaris. I've no idea how she knows where we are. I've no idea if we really are anywhere, but we struggle on as best as we can, cutting our way through the dense growth. I'm carrying the Elvish sword Makri gave me, the weapon she won at the great sword-fighting tournament. It's a fine blade and it makes my life a little easier. Makri has a sword in each hand, one Elvish and one Orcish. Her twin-sword fighting technique, almost unknown in the west, has proved devastatingly effective in combat, but she still struggles to cut through the huge swathe of trees, bushes, and vines that surround us on all sides. Eventually we come to a halt.

'There's no getting through this,' says Lisutaris.

'Can you use a spell?'

'I was trying to preserve my magic.' Our Commander is capable of storing a vast amount of sorcery, using spell after spell when necessary, but even she has a limit. Once it's used up, it takes time to recharge. She scowls as a vine tries to wrap itself round her neck.

'To hell with this,' she mutters, and raises one hand. There's a flash of blue light and the vegetation in front of her shrivels and withers, leaving a broad clear path for us to advance. It's a great improvement, and we hurry along.

'There's something shining in the distance,' says Makri, whose eyesight is extremely keen, thanks to her Elvish blood.

'That will be the way out. Can you see anything else?'

'Some bears.'

'Bears? They'd better get out the way if they know what's good for them.' Lisutaris hasn't enjoyed our arduous journey. She's capable of physical exertion, but it's rather beneath her, and not something she's used to. As we approach the shining gate, the bears examine us with interest. They're large creatures, and seem like they might be about to attack. However, at the sight of one angry sorcerer, one bodyguard with two swords in her hands, and a bad-tempered investigator, they decide against it, and vanish in a puff of purple smoke.

'Just as well for them. I'm in no mood for hostile bears.' Lisutaris examines the structure in front of us. 'This gate will take us out of the magic space, close to the temple. The High Priestess will be waiting.'

'I hope your oracle is worth it.'

'It will be.' Lisutaris sounds confident. Her faith in this High Priestess appears to be unshakable. Foolish, in my opinion, but she's the Commander.

'I think someone might be following us,' says Makri.

'Following us?' I turn round. There's no one in sight. Just a long stretch of vegetation, shrivelled from Lisutaris's spell but already growing back.

'I thought I saw some sort of shadow. I thought I saw it behind us on the mountain too.'

Lisutaris gazes into the distance. 'I don't think we could be followed through the magic space,' she says, eventually. 'No one even knows we're here.'

No one actually expresses the notion that there seem to be no limits to what Deeziz the Unseen can do, but we're probably all thinking the same. Our Commander leads us through the gate, back into the real world. While our journey seemed both lengthy and hazardous, in reality we've only travelled about a mile from camp.

143

We trudge through the darkness towards a small copse of trees. I'm straining my eyes as we advance, wary of Orcish attack. Thanks to the inefficiency of Hanama's intelligence unit, we have no idea where the Orcish army is. Current opinion among our generals is divided, some of them believing Prince Amrag and his troops have remained in Turai, waiting for us. Others believe they've probably advanced, and may even be close to the Simnian border. If Deeziz has really completed her grand hiding spell, they could be right next to us. I'm prepared for the worst.

I shiver. It's a cold night and there's moisture in the air. The thick clouds are low overhead, obscuring the moons and the stars. When we enter the trees at the foot of the hill we can hardly see a yard in front of our faces. Makri leads the way, her swords drawn. She halts, and points.

'We're here.'

I'm struggling to make out anything in the gloom. Eventually I manage to distinguish a marble pillar. Somewhere behind it there's a tiny flicker of flame. We advance. More pillars come into view. We're in the middle of an old, ruined temple. The roof has collapsed, leaving only the ivy-covered pillars and an altar, on which burns a very small fire. At the altar stands the High Priestess. She looks exactly the same as the last time we saw her. Elderly, grey-haired, tall and dignified. A suspicious character in every way.

Lisutaris strides forward and bows. For a moment I'm worried she might start heaping more gold on the High Priestess, possibly feeling that the king's ransom she handed over before might not have been enough. That doesn't happen. They greet each other quietly. There are a few moments of silence. Then the High Priestess, perhaps feeling that her business would be best concluded swiftly, speaks softly to Lisutaris.

'Advance into the clouds.'

Lisutaris nods. 'Thank you, High Priestess. I am greatly honoured that you travelled here to give me this oracle.'

The High Priestess turns to leave. Seeing this, I'm unable to fully contain myself. I try, but I can't entirely suppress a grunt of frustration at the thought of the arduous journey we've endured for yet another worthless piece of advice. Advance into the clouds indeed.

Rather to my surprise, the High Priestess halts, turns round, and takes a step towards us. She's a few inches taller than me and gazes down at me in a manner I don't much like.

'You regard Lisutaris's consulting me as a waste of time.'

'I do.'

'Please ignore him,' says Lisutaris.

The Priestess stares at me. 'You didn't like the oracle you received.'

'Of course I didn't like it. The day will never come when I thrown down my shield and flee.'

The High Priestess smiles faintly. 'We shall see.' Once more she turns to leave.

'Why don't you tell me something useful,' I call after her. 'Like where Tirini's shoes are.' I'm not certain why I ask that. I suppose Tirini's shoes have been on my mind.

'Captain Thraxas, I order you to be quiet,' says Lisutaris. 'I'm sorry, High Priestess, this man is—'

The High Priestess turns her head. 'New shoes can hide old shoes,' she says. And with that, she disappears into the darkness. Presumably she has some attendants, waiting to take her home. Or perhaps she has some sorcerous means of travel, I wouldn't know. Either way, it's the last we see of her.

'Captain Thraxas, I won't stand for this insolence,' says Lisutaris, angrily. 'When we get back—'

'There's something overhead,' says Makri, urgently.

'What?'

We scan the skies, but can see nothing in the dark clouds. I draw my sword. I have a very bad feeling about everything. Suddenly the air is split by a terrible screech. It's a sound I know; the sound of a war dragon diving to attack. A dark shape emerges from the cloud and plunges towards us, its wings beating furiously. Lisutaris raises her hands, ready to strike it with a spell but before she can summon up her power the dragon vanishes behind the tops of the trees.

'Why didn't it attack?'

'Maybe it was just offloading something,' I suggest. Suddenly the earth vibrates and there's a noise that sounds like a tree crashing to the ground.

'Offloading something that can uproot trees.'

We make ready to fight.

Chapter Nineteen

We're standing with our backs to the altar. In front of us are several ancient pillars. There's a short space between the pillars and the trees. Into this space stride six heavily-armed Orcs. Behind them comes the largest two-legged creature I've ever seen. Some sort of troll, perhaps, but much bigger. Three times the height of a man, at least. It has legs and arms like tree trunks and it's carrying a gigantic metal mace that looks as if could knock down a building. It flashes briefly through my mind that such a troll is impossible. No human-shaped creature can grow that big. Its muscles wouldn't support it. It's a very brief thought however, because this creature's muscles seem to be supporting it just fine. It strides towards us, swinging its huge mace, following the Orcish warriors.

Out of the corner of my eye I notice a purple light. Lisutaris hasn't wasted any time summoning up a spell. Her eyes turn purple, sparks flicker around her hands and she sends a blast of visible energy towards the troll. The creature halts, snarls, shakes its head, then keeps on coming. Lisutaris has just struck it with the sort of sorcery she uses to bring down dragons, and it hasn't stopped it.

'Hit it again!' I yell.

Lisutaris shakes her head. She used a lot of sorcery getting us through the magic space. I'm guessing she won't be able to summon up another powerful spell like that for a while. By now the Orcs are upon us. Makri engages them. I shove Lisutaris back against the altar where we can protect her, and rush to Makri's side.

'I knew that priestess would be the death of us. Damned oracles.'

Makri has already dispatched one of her opponents, killing an Orc with a deft thrust to the throat, delivered through a tiny gap in his armour, the sort of stroke that only she can make. I slip my small shield onto my left arm and do my best to ward off the opponent on my left while hewing at the one in front. I may not be as skilled as Makri but I have a lot of fighting experience. My blade hacks into his sword arm. As he lurches backwards I stab him again in his unprotected shin and he falls, not dead, but out of the fight, which is just as good. I use my shield to deflect a heavy blow from my left while Makri simultaneously parries one Orc's sword and another's spear. She darts forward to plant her black Orcish blade under the armpit of the Orc with the spear, sending it deep into his chest. He falls down dead. In the space of a few seconds we've killed or disabled three of our six adversaries. You might say we were doing well, were it not for the gigantic troll who now decides it's time he joined the fight. He strides forward, pushes the three remaining Orcs roughly aside, and swings his mace at us in a great arc. It moves a lot faster than you might have expected, given his size. Makri and I throw ourselves backwards. The mace, a huge chunk of metal, crashes into one of the old marble pillars and it crumples under the impact. Shards of marble hit me in the face. Without pausing, the vast troll, clearly enhanced by some sort of dire sorcery, sweeps his mace back down in another arc. Makri and I are driven back, right up against the altar.

'Any chance of another spell?' I cry.

'No,' says Lisutaris. She draws her short sword, for all the good that will do. The troll raises the mace again. I grab Lisutaris and throw her over the altar, and follow her as quickly as I can. We make it just in time. The troll's mace smashes into the altar, breaking it into pieces. I find myself on my back, looking over a pile of shattered marble. Makri, it turns out, didn't follow us over the altar. She took the opportunity to duck under the mace and attack. She manages to plant her sword in the creature's shin. It's a brave manoeuvre. Unfortunately it has no effect. The troll doesn't even seem to feel it. To make matters worse, Makri's sword gets stuck. It takes her only a second to pull it free but it's enough time for the troll to kick out at her. Makri is sent flying backwards by the force of the blow. She lands beside us, dazed and bleeding. The troll advances. Behind it come the three remaining Orcish warriors. The situation is looking bad.

I have to get the troll away from Lisutaris. If our War Leader dies here, the west will fall to Prince Amrag. On the ground beside me is small bowl of incense, still burning. I stand up, pick up the bowl, and fling it at the troll. I have no great hopes of this, but it does distract it for a second. I leap forward, invert my sword, and jam it down with all my strength on the beast's smallest toe, visible through its enormous sandals. Whether because of my bulk and strength, or perhaps some weakness of the toes, this does produce an effect. The gigantic troll howls in pain, and rounds on me, a look of demented fury on its face.

'How d'you like that?' I cry, and jam my sword back into its toe. This produces another howl of rage, and a swing of the mace that would break me into pieces were it to connect. Having now caught the monster's attention, I set off at a run, hurling curses and abuse as I go. If I can just distract the troll for long enough, Lisutaris might be able to come up with something. Or else she can flee. Makri can surely take care of the three remaining Orcs.

I run through the trees, down a slope. I glance back over my shoulder and am horrified to see that the troll is gaining on me. I'm not the fastest runner in the world - being rather bulky for this sort of exercise - but I had thought I might outpace it. Apparently not. Whoever made this magic troll gave it a lot of speed. It's gaining on me. I discard my shield, in an effort to run faster. It doesn't really help. I can sense that at any moment I'm going to be flattened by the largest mace ever seen in the west. I risk another glance over my shoulder. The troll is right behind me. Its weapon is in the air, swinging towards me. At this vital moment, I catch my foot on a tree root and crash to the ground. A look of bestial pleasure appears on the troll's face as it prepares to squash me like a bug.

'Damn you!' I cry, from the ground, as it looms over me. In rage and frustration, I fling my sword at its face. To my absolute astonishment, my Elvish blade goes right into the troll's eye, sinking in deep and true. The huge creature halts, shudders, then falls to the ground. I haul myself to my feet, unable quite to believe what just happened. Swords aren't designed to be thrown accurately like that. I couldn't do it again if my life depended on it. Yet here we are, one dead troll and one live investigator, feeling pleased with himself.

I remove my sword from the troll's eye. The sharp Elvish blade penetrated very deeply I must express my gratitude to the Elves some time. Wearily, I make my way back up the hill. I'm worn out, and can't move very quickly. If Makri and Lisutaris can't deal with the remaining Orcs, I'm not going to get there in time to help. Towards the top of the slope, I pick up my discarded shield, and trudge on. When I arrive back at the shattered altar I find Makri standing over the bodies of three dead Orcs. Lisutaris is by her side. Very incongruously, Makri grins.

'What are you smiling about?'

'You will throw down your shield and flee.'

I look at my shield. I did discard it, I suppose.

'I told you it might not be such a bad oracle,' says Lisutaris.

'That High Priestess really knows her business,' says Makri. 'I wonder when I'm becoming queen?'

I'm no longer sure what I think about the High Priestess's utterances. I wonder what she meant by *new shoes can hide old shoes*. I'd like to think about that, though there's no time to ponder it now.

Lisutaris is studying the huge troll. 'I've never seen anything like this.'

'Presumably Deeziz made it.'

'It was sorcerously enhanced, obviously,' says Makri. 'A humanoid can't grow that big, not naturally anyway. It's muscles wouldn't support it. The square-cube law means that as the body grows, the strength required for–'

'I already knew that,' I say, interrupting.

Makri looks offended. 'You might have let me finish.'

I turn to Lisutaris. 'I told you this was a bad idea. Deeziz must have followed us. She's ambushed us again. You were almost killed.'

'I have complete confidence in my Bodyguard and Chief Security Officer. You protected me, didn't you?'

'We were lucky.'

'I disagree. We coped with adversity. And now, having received my oracle, we have to get back as quickly as possible.' Lisutaris produces her magic purse. She expands the purse's mouth till it's once more large enough to step into.

I stare at it without enthusiasm. 'Do we have to go through that thing again? We're not that far from camp, we could walk.'

150

'We need to get back there instantly,' says the sorcerer. 'We'll be travelling faster this time.'

'Faster? You mean like Tirini when she almost killed herself?'

'Yes.'

'Any reason to think it won't kill us?'

'I'm more powerful than Tirini.'

'Normally. But you've used up all your sorcery.'

'Captain Thraxas, stop complaining and get into the purse. Ensign Makri, prepare for a rapid journey.'

I doubt that Makri's much keener than I am to take another excursion through the magic space but she doesn't protest. We follow Lisutaris back into the magic space.

'Do we have to take the same route–' I begin, but I don't get any further. Lisutaris snaps her fingers and we're immediately dragged through the air at incredible speed, a journey so rapid that it's almost impossible to see where we're going. Raindrops pound against my face like rocks. We go down the side of a mountain like an avalanche. At one point I think I bounce off a troll. In less than a minute I find myself lying face down on the ground, aching everywhere.

'We're back,' says Lisutaris, also face down on the ground.

'I think I might have gone through the talking pig,' says Makri.

We haul ourselves to our feet. I glare at Lisutaris. 'That was terrible. It's a miracle we survived.'

'And yet we did.'

Nearby is a familiar glowing oval; the door to the real world. Before leading us through, Lisutaris surveys the terrain behind us. She asks Makri if she can see anyone following us. Makri shakes her head, but in the ever-shifting colours and changing landscape around us, it's impossible for her to be certain.

'If Deeziz has been following us, perhaps I can keep her in here for a little while. Be prepared to move quickly.'

Lisutaris sweeps one hand through the air while chanting a brief spell in an arcane language. Fire begins to consume the landscape, spreading so swiftly in every direction that we're obliged to sprint towards the exit and throw ourselves through. I land painfully on my face, back in our War Leader's command tent. Makri lands on top of me. Lisutaris emerges in a more dignified manner. When I look up at her magic purse, flames are licking around the portal to the magic space. She snaps it shut.

'If Deeziz the Unseen was in there, that will give her something to think about.'

'Will it kill her?' I haul myself to my feet.

'No. But it will close all the nearest exits. It might delay her return for a short time. A short time I intend to use.' I'm expecting to sit down and rest while Lisutaris summons servants to bring us wine, possibly pausing to congratulate me on my bravery against the gigantic troll. None of that happens.

'Follow me,' says Lisutaris, curtly, and strides from the tent.

Outside, the weather has worsened. Clouds still cover the moons. The rain has intensified. In the distance there's the dull rumble of thunder. The guards outside salute Lisutaris as she emerges. She turns and gazes to the east, though it's difficult to make out anything in the gloom.

'Makri,' she says. 'Am I right in thinking that the clouds are touching the tops of those hills?'

Makri, sharp-eyed, nods. 'They are.'

'Very good.' She addresses her guards. 'Summon my messengers immediately.' Two of the guards hurry off. Lisutaris has an array of young messengers, mostly human, though there are a few Elves among them. They sleep nearby in case she needs them quickly. They're used to having their sleep interrupted and they tumble out of their tents quickly enough, hurrying towards us while still fastening their clothes. Lisutaris addresses them in low but urgent tones.

'I want every Commander and Deputy-Commander here, instantly. Tell them it's urgent and there must be no delay.'

The young messengers salute briskly and hurry off, fanning out through the slumbering camp towards the tents of the various military commanders.

'What's happening?' I ask.

'Advance into the clouds,' mutters our War Leader.

I look at her in surprise. 'You mean right away?'

'Yes.'

152

'Are you sure that's what the oracle meant?'

'We'll soon find out,' replies the sorcerer. 'You'd better fetch your unit, you'll be accompanying me.'

I'm not convinced this is the greatest plan ever formulated but there's no point arguing if Lisutaris has made up her mind. I hurry back to my wagon where I waken Droo, Anumaris and Rinderan.

'You've got about thirty seconds to get ready,' I tell them. 'We're going into action.'

'Is the enemy close?' asks Rinderan, alarmed.

'Possibly. I don't really know.'

We still have no information as to the whereabouts of Prince Amrag. Disregarding our lack of knowledge, Lisutaris apparently intends to lead our army into the clouds, just because the High Priestess recommended it. I open a bottle of beer, take a good drink, then hand it to Droo. Droo drinks and hands it to Anumaris. Unusually, the young sorcerer accepts it, and drinks.

'Everyone got their sword, shield, and whatever else you need? Fine, let's go.'

We hurry back towards Lisutaris's command tent. By now a series of sleepy and bad-tempered commanders have begun to arrive, none of them thrilled at being dragged from their beds on a cold, rainy night. Bishop-General Ritari and Legate Apiroi are there, accompanied by two black-clad Niojan generals who've only just arrived in camp with their troops. I'm not even sure if Lisutaris has properly conferred with the Niojans yet. She beckons everyone into her tent. There's some confusion as they all enter, some yawning and muttering. Even though it's obvious that important events are about to happen, I notice the Niojan generals looking askance at Makri. People often do, when they notice her Orcish blood for the first time. The Elvish commanders aren't exactly comfortable in her presence either, though they've had time to get used to her. Among the crowd of generals and their subordinates is Hanama. I might have known she'd force her way in somehow.

Lisutaris holds up her hand, bringing the muttering to a halt. For a woman who's recently made two difficult journeys through the magic space, she's looking in good condition. I can't say the same for either Makri or me, both of whom look like we've gone several rounds with a dragon. Whether it's Lisutaris's natural aristocratic bearing, or whether she worked a quick spell on herself when no one was looking, I can't say, but she stands in front of the crowd looking authoritative, composed, and commanding.

'Gentlemen,' she begins. 'It's time to advance. We head east immediately, in battle formation.'

The silence is shattered by a welter of raised voices.

'What? Have we found the Orcish Army?'

'Is Prince Amrag close?'

'What's our plan? When are we leaving?'

'We're leaving as soon as possible,' says Lisutaris. 'I want the army to advance fifteen minutes after you leave this tent.'

'We've only just got here,' protests one of the Niojan Generals. 'Our men are tired. We've had no time to rehearse any tactics with the rest of the troops.'

'You've been in battle before. The Niojans will take the left flank. The Simnians and Elves the right. I will advance with the Samsarinans in the centre.'

'What about our baggage train? asks General Hemistos. 'It'll take hours to secure it properly.

'We'll leave it unsecured,' replies Lisutaris.

None of the generals look happy about this. Like any army, we have a lot of baggage. The wagons and non-combatants who follow the soldiers are carrying supplies, supplies without which the army couldn't survive. Leaving them unprotected is unusual, and seems rash. If we advance, find nothing, and then arrive back to find our supplies destroyed, we'll practically be defeated before we've even been in a fight.

Bishop-General Ritari points out that he hasn't had time to properly assign all of his cavalry units.

'Then do it now,' says Lisutaris, calmly. 'Send your cavalry and light infantry along our flanks, deploying whichever units you see fit. Use your initiative.'

Legate Apiroi, the Niojan politician, isn't looking happy. 'Why are we taking this impetuous action? We have no information as to the whereabouts of the Orcish army.'

'You have no information regarding the Orcish army,' retorts Lisutaris. 'But you're not War Leader. I am. Prepare to advance.'

'What if we advance right into a trap?' asks the Samsarinan General Mexes. If Prince Amrag encircles us in the dark, we'll be destroyed.'

It's a reasonable question, and a point that's been on my mind. I can envisage us advancing blindly over the top of a hill right into a regiment of Orcish phalanxes, concealed by a grand hiding spell, ready to assault us from both sides. If that happens, and our army isn't fully prepared - which it won't be - then disaster will overwhelm us. Our War Leader will listen to no arguments. She quietens the generals and the politicians, and instructs them to get ready. 'We advance in battle formation in fifteen minutes. I expect your units to be ready. If they're not, I'll be appointing new officers. Dismissed.'

The commanders troop out of the tent. None of them look that enthusiastic. Lisutaris lights a thazis stick.

'Are we advancing with the troops?' asks Makri.

'We are,' says Lisutaris. 'I don't have time to fully deploy the Sorcerers Regiment among the rest of the army so they'll all be following me in the middle.' Makri looks pleased. As for me, I don't mind that I'm going to be in the thick of things. Gurd will probably be pleased too: the Sorcerers Auxiliary Regiment will be marching right in front of Lisutaris, so he'll be close to the action.

Lisutaris's aide-de-camp Julius informs her that the sorcerers are now gathering outside.

'Show them in. The Sorcerers Regiment is in for some front-line fighting, earlier than expected.'

Chapter Twenty

Twenty five minutes later I'm marching up a hill in almost complete darkness. The rain is pouring down, the wind is picking up, and I've no idea where I'm going. Over a hill, obviously, but what we'll meet on the other side, I don't know. Lisutaris sent Hanama and her team on ahead with orders to report back if they find anything. As they haven't been particularly successful in finding anything up till now, I don't expect this time will be any different. Either the Orcish army is miles away, or Deeziz the Unseen has managed to hide them so efficiently that we won't notice anything till they're crashing into us. I don't even know if our troops are marching in proper formation. The newly-arrived Niojan army is meant to be on our left flank but I can't see them. All torches have been extinguished by order of our War Leader, and she's instructed the army to march in silence. No trumpets sound, and no one shouts orders. The wind and rain muffle our footsteps as we advance.

I'm not altogether impressed with this development. Our army is not yet prepared for complicated manoeuvres in the dark. If we end up with huge gaps between the Niojans on the left, the Samsarinans in the middle and the Elves and Simnians on the right, no one will be surprised. Not too far ahead of us is Gurd, and I know he'll have his doubts too. Both of us have advanced in uncertain conditions in the past and we're both experienced enough to know that things can easily go wrong. If we're ambushed in the dark we'll be massacred. Some sorcerers have been sent to the front, using their powers to mask our advance, but whether they can hide us from the powerful Orcish sorcerers remains to be seen.

Before we reach the top of the hill I feel the temperature drop and the air turn damper. Visibility drops to almost zero. We've advanced into the clouds, as the High Priestess advised. I notice that Droo is looking nervous. She's never been in action before. As an Elvish scout, I doubt she'd have been expecting to find herself in the midst of a full-scale battle. It will be the same all over the army. We left camp so quickly there was no time to organise ourselves properly. The leading phalanxes are all more-or-less in

156

position but elsewhere, units have just had to fit in where they can. Samsarinan armoured troops march alongside Elvish bowmen while lightly-armoured skirmishers, more used to being on the flanks, find themselves beside heavily-armoured troops with bronze breastplates and shields. Neither are our sorcerers as well distributed as they should be. Normally there would be more on the flanks and some assigned to the rear, but most of them are close to Lisutaris, just ahead of me. It's not the organised advance one would have wished for. I hope we don't come to regret it.

Despite her nerves, Droo is bearing up well enough, aided by the flask of klee she produces from beneath her dull green tunic. She takes a sip and passes it to me. I gulp some down. It burns my throat.

'Good klee,' I whisper.

'Stole it from the Niojans,' she whispers back.

I pass the flask to Anumaris Thunderbolt. I doubt she'd normally drink klee, but she sips a little of the fiery spirit, wincing as it trickles down her throat, then passes it to Rinderan. The young sorcerer from the Southern Hills seems to be bearing up well enough, given that he's never been in military action before. The ground levels off. We're at the top of the hill, in the clouds. I'm suddenly gripped by a strong feeling of doom. Deeziz the Unseen has fooled us, tricked Lisutaris somehow. We're going to march down the hill and find Orcish battalions waiting for us right and left. We'll be encircled, caught in the middle and massacred, half our troops crushed to death without ever landing a blow. I shake my head. I suppose a final battle with the Orcs isn't such a bad way to go. It's what I've been expecting for the past fifteen years. I'd have liked better weather. I'm already as wet as a mermaid's blanket, and walking through the low-lying clouds isn't helping.

We start to descend, advancing in tense silence through the gloom. The wind and rain still mask our presence. The slope becomes steeper. The cloud thins a little. I can just make out two shadowy figures ahead, approaching Lisutaris. Hanama and her Elvish assassin companion. They whisper something in our War Leader's ear then disappear again. Lisutaris mutters something to her young messengers. They hurry off. I notice that Makri is drawing her swords. Seconds later, our trumpets sound the charge. The army responds immediately. There's a great roar as we run down the hill, through the darkness, with no idea what awaits us.

It suddenly strikes me what the High Priestess meant when she said "new shoes can hide old shoes." Of course. Now I know who Deeziz is. I wonder if I'll survive to tell anyone.

As the army cascades downwards we pick up a lot of momentum. We burst out of the cloud cover as the first, faint streaks of dawn appear in the sky. Just ahead of us there's a long string of flickering torches, like a procession. Carrying the torches are thousands of Orcs. Unfortunately for them, they're not in battle formation. They're not even facing us. They're marching round the foot of the hill, and we've caught them side-on, unprepared for our assault. The Samsarinan and Turanian phalanxes at the head of our army plough straight into their unprotected flank. The Orcs, with no time to get in formation, are cut down by the spears of our phalanxes, then trampled underfoot as we surge over them. Their line crumples with almost no resistance. Orcs scream and flee, only to be caught up in the confused mass of Orcs behind them. None of them has enough time or space to organise any sort of defence. Our phalanxes sweep them away. By the time I reach the foot of the hill, there's not a living Orc in sight, though plenty of dead are strewn around. As far as the eye can see, to right and left, the same thing has happened. The Orcish army was in the very process of mounting a sneak attack on our army. Unfortunately for them, we got our sneak attack in first. We've broken them in pieces. My mind flashes back to the time Prince Amrag's forces smashed into the unprepared Turanian army. We crumpled like a sheet of parchment, with heavy casualties. This time, we've done it to them.

The sky is now lit up with the brilliant illumination of sorcerous fire, as our Sorcerers Guild presses home our advantage. I catch sight of a few Eastern sorcerers, fighting back desperately, but they're as unprepared as every other Orc, and they're cut down quickly by the massed ranks around Lisutaris. We've severed the Orcish line in multiple places. Each part of their broken army is in full retreat, surrounded on three sides by the encircling attackers as the Niojans sweep in from the left and the Simnians and Elves from the right. Many Orcs die without even being able to draw their weapons, crushed by weight of their panicking comrades. It's common in battle to have little idea of what's going on, but here, even in the dim light of the approaching dawn, it's plain to see that Lisutaris has scored a stunning victory over the previously invincible Prince Amrag. His army has been routed, with great slaughter. Casualties among our troops are very light.

Some battles go on for hours. This one was effectively over in minutes. Once an enemy has been routed as thoroughly as the Orcs have been, there's no coming back. It was so quick that I hardly saw any action. There's some blood on my sword, but only because I dispatched a wounded Orc who was lying on the ground. Both Droo and Anumaris are excited by our victory. Droo is about to chase after the remnants of the fleeing Orcs but I hold her back. Pursuit can be left to those mounted troops who specialise in it. Even now they'll be mopping up remnants of our enemies. As Lisutaris's security detail, we should remain close to her. I lead my unit towards the sorcerers, many of whom are still massed around Lisutaris. Some of them are still projecting protective shields around our leader, while others have halted, to recharge their magic. I find Makri, standing on her own, not far from Lisutaris. I embrace her. She's surprised. So am I.

'Why did you do that?'

I shrug. I hadn't been planning on embracing her. It just happened. Makri gives me a suspicious look. Despite our victory, she doesn't seem that happy. 'I hardly saw any fighting. They all ran away before I could get there.'

'Best kind of battle,' I tell her. 'I need to talk to Lisutaris.'

'She's busy with her generals.'

'I still need to talk to her.'

I march forward. Curious as to my intentions, Makri, Droo and Anumaris follow on. In the immediate aftermath of battle, messengers and junior officers are hurrying to and fro, carrying orders and bringing reports from the units in the field. Elves and humans, some on foot and some on horseback, hurry in every direction. There's a degree of elation in the air after our victory, but one battle doesn't make a war, and there are still plenty of decisions to be made. Lisutaris is deep in conversation with her most senior commanders and sorcerers. As I approach her, one of her personal staff holds out his arm, barring my way.

'Can't disturb the Commander at the moment,' he says.

I bat him out the way. He grabs hold of me as I pass. I keep on going. Another staff officer grabs my tunic, trying to prevent me from approaching Lisutaris. I keep on going. I've got a lot of bulk and we're on a downward slope. I'm a hard man to stop. I barge past a general I don't recognise, still with two junior officers trying to pull me back. There's quite a lot of shouting. Lisutaris, in conversation with General Hemistos, looks up.

'What's going on?'

'I need to talk to you.'

'It'll have to wait,' snaps Lisutaris, and turns back to Hemistos.

'Can't wait,' I say, and grab her arm. At this there's the sound of swords being drawn as Lisutaris's outraged staff officers prepare to cut me down for insubordination.

'Captain Thraxas!' roars Lisutaris, outraged at my effrontery.

I lean forward to whisper in her ear. 'I know who Deeziz is. I'd guess you have about thirty seconds to catch her before she flees so I suggest you get the magic purse out and get us back to camp.'

Our War Leader stares at me for a second. 'Damn you Thraxas, if this is a false alarm I'll have you executed.'

'We've probably got twenty seconds left.'

Lisutaris turns to General Hemistos. 'Take charge while I'm gone.' With that, she whips out her magic purse and mutters the required words, opening an oval portal of light. She steps into it, followed by Makri. I grab Anumaris and Droo, one in each hand, and step into the light.

160

Chapter Twenty-One

Our first two journeys through the magic space were bad enough. The third is worse, though mercifully brief. As Lisutaris leads us through it's cold, frightening, and I feel like I'm about to die. I see unpleasant shapes and hear dreadful noises that I could never describe again. When we emerge back at our camp, none of us look in good shape.

'I didn't know you could travel so fast in the magic space,' mutters Anumaris, sinking to her knees. Makri is shivering. Even the effervescent Droo looks like she might be sick. Lisutaris, no longer as elegant and upright, turns to me.

'Well?'

'This way.'

Anumaris needs time to recover. We leave her where she is. I lead the others behind Lisutaris's command tent. A few non-combatants, unaware of events on the battlefield, bombard us with questions.

'What happened?' cries a young woman, a Samsarinan cook.

'We won,' replies Droo, but doesn't manage to sound very happy about it. It'll take a while for the effects of our emergency journey through the magic space to wear off. I halt outside the tent housing the ailing Tirini Snake Smiter.

'In here.'

I march in, and almost bump into Saabril Clearwater, Medical Sorcerer, First Class. We come to an abrupt halt, face to face. I take a step back. Saabril nods to me politely, and greets Lisutaris.

'You can drop the fake Kamaran accent,' I tell her. 'And the fake appearance too. I know you're Deeziz the Unseen.'

I turn to my companions with an expression of triumph on my face. There's nothing like a dramatic revelation to make an investigator feel good. It always impresses the clients. Facing me in a semi-circle are Lisutaris, Makri and Droo. I can't help noticing none of them are looking impressed.

'Saabril Clearwater is Deeziz the Unseen?' Lisutaris sounds sceptical.

'Yes.'

'I don't think she is. I can't see any trace of identity concealment.'

'That's because she's really good at it.'

'But I'm the greatest sorcerer in the west.'

'And she's the greatest sorcerer in the east!'

'We did check her out carefully,' says Droo. 'We didn't find anything suspicious.'

'Of course you didn't. She's the Head of the Orcish Sorcerer's Guild! She fooled us.'

Anumaris Thunderbolt arrives, still looking pale. 'What's happening?'

'Thraxas thinks Saabril Clearwater is Deeziz the Unseen.'

'But we checked her out. We didn't find anything suspicious.'

'Then maybe you didn't check her carefully enough!' I cry, becoming frustrated.

Tirini Snake Smiter is lying on a camp bed in the corner, apparently sleeping. Saabril glances at her before addressing Lisutaris. 'I'm sure Captain Thraxas has good reasons for what he's saying. But really, I'm not Deeziz. I'm sorry to have caused any confusion.'

'It's no use standing there being polite! I know you're Deeziz! You were about to flee!'

'No I wasn't.'

There seem to be no signs of imminent flight. She isn't carrying a bag or anything like that. There's a half-drunk goblet of wine on the small wooden table, and an open scroll.

'All right, I may have been wrong about the fleeing part. But only because she thinks she's too smart for us. She's still Deeziz.' Somehow this isn't sounding as convincing as I imagined it would. Lisutaris taps her foot on the ground impatiently. 'Captain Thraxas, I do have a war to fight...'

'She's Deeziz and I can prove it!'

'How?'

'With language! Her name is Deeziz. When she appeared in Turai she called herself Moolifi. And now she's called Saabril. You see the connection?'

162

Lisutaris, Droo and Anumaris look blank, but Makri nods. 'You mean the double vowels, with an "I" coming later?'

'Yes. Deeziz, Moolifi, Saabril. Names all constructed the same way.'

'Not exactly the same way,' says Lisutaris.

'Well they're very similar!'

Lisutaris turns to Makri. 'Is this significant?'

'The vowel digraphs? I don't know. I suppose it could be. Some sub-conscious connection while choosing a new identity.'

Lisutaris stares hard at Saabril, trying to pick up any sign that she might not be who she says she is. The young Kamaran sorcerer looks back at her quite calmly. With her fair skin and long fair hair, she looks to be exactly who she says she is.

'Captain Thraxas,' says Lisutaris. 'I'm not convinced. Is that the only evidence you have?'

'There's more. She stole Tirini's shoes.'

Anumaris raises her eyebrows. 'Tirini's shoes?'

Lisutaris sighs. 'Thraxas has become obsessed with them.' You can tell her faith in me is rapidly declining, and I'm not sure it was ever that high in the first place.

'Tirini's shoes have a special sorcerous power! They can hide a person's past. That's what the High Priestess meant when she said "New shoes can hide old shoes."'

'You don't believe in the High Priestess,' objects Lisutaris.

'She may not be the total fool I imagined. Tirini wasn't called Tirini when she was born, she was called Tirina. She was the daughter of a sewer inspector. Somehow she got hold of a pair of magic shoes which were specially designed to hide a person's background. She used them to hide her poor origins when she went to the Sorcerers College. She's kept them ever since because she doesn't want anyone to know about her family.'

At this, Tirini opens her eyes. She glares at me. 'None of this is true.'

'It is true! That's why we could never find Deeziz! She added the power of Tirini's shoes to her own sorcery. It was enough to hide her background, and baffle any sort of spell or enquiry.

Meanwhile she's been making Tirini sicker so she won't ask for her shoes back.'

'Thraxas is talking nonsense,' says Tirini. 'Daughter of a sewer inspector indeed.'

Saabril Clearwater holds up her hands, protesting her innocence. 'I really don't know what Captain Thraxas is talking about.'

'She's probably wearing the shoes right now!' I cry. 'Orange slippers, I believe.' I point triumphantly at Saabril's feet. Unfortunately she's wearing a pair of standard issue Sorcerer's Regiment army boots. Our War Leader glares at me with a face like thunder.

'She could have hidden them with a spell,' I protest.

There's quite a long pause.

'Lisutaris, this woman just followed us through the magic space and back again. You must have some sort of spell for verifying that?'

'I don't.'

'You don't have any means of telling if someone's just been in the magic space?'

'No.'

'Why not?'

'There isn't a spell for everything.'

'We really did research Saabril Clearwater's background very carefully,' says Anumaris.

I'm struggling to think what to say next when Makri steps forward. 'It's strange,' she says.

'What's strange?' asks Lisutaris.

'It's strange that Thraxas is usually right about this sort of thing. Because he's such a fool about everything else.'

With that, Makri unsheathes her silver Elvish sword at lightning speed and aims a scything stroke at Saabril's neck. The sorcerer reacts instantly. There's a flash of light and Makri is thrown back against the side of the tent. Saabril is no longer here. Instead we find ourselves facing a familiar figure; Deeziz the Unseen, looking exactly the same as the last time we encountered her in Turai, moments before she brought down the north wall and let in the Orcish army. She raises her arm but before she can utter a spell

164

Lisutaris leaps forward and catches her hand. They stand, face to face, hands locked, purple sparks flying from their fingers as they strive for dominance.

When an enemy sorcerer is engaged in magic, distracted by an opponent, it's often possible to deal them a lot of damage in a conventional manner. I attempt to do just that, taking out my sword and thrusting it towards Deeziz's ribs. As I fly back against the side of the tent, howling in pain from the agonising shockwave that surges up my arm, I reflect that this tactic obviously doesn't work against a sorcerer as powerful as Deeziz. I find myself sprawled next to Makri. We watch as the two most powerful sorcerers in the world struggle to gain an advantage. They're still locked together, their brows knitted in concentration, sparks and flames leaking from their fingers as they battle for supremacy. There's every chance that the tent will catch fire but at the moment, I can't move. As I watch, Anumaris attempts to join in, but the spell she casts rebounds straight back on her. She wails in pain, and ends up on the ground beside us. Droo is notching an arrow in her bow. I could tell her that it's not going to help, but the pain in my arm makes it difficult to speak.

Lisutaris's face is only inches from Deeziz's. 'I know you now. You'll never hide from me again.'

'You won't survive to search for me.'

The light around them intensifies. Droo fires her arrow at Deeziz. It doesn't even graze her. Instead it turns round, flies back towards the young Elf, and buries itself in her shoulder. Droo winces in pain then sits down, injured and disappointed.

The flames and sparks intensify. I really think the tent might catch fire. I attempt to haul myself to my feet. Maybe if I just hurl myself at Deeziz my bulk might put her off for a second, allowing Lisutaris a brief advantage. We need to do something, because Lisutaris, while holding her own, isn't showing any signs of winning. In fact, I'd say that Deeziz is looking stronger. To my surprise, Tirini raises herself in her sick bed. She looks desperately ill, but I do notice a determined expression settle over her features. She raises one hand in the air, pointing towards Deeziz. A blast of purple light catches the Orcish sorcerer right in the back, causing

165

her to stagger. Lisutaris immediately takes advantage. The light around her hands intensifies and sparks flow into Deeziz. Her hair flows outwards as if caught in a strong breeze as she's battered by Lisutaris from one side and Tirini from the other. Even so, they can't finish her off. The Head of the Orcish Sorcerers Guild rises a few inches in the air. A large orange oval of light appears beside her. When she speaks, she manages to sound calm, despite being under furious assault.

'Until next time, Lisutaris, Mistress of the Sky.'

With that, Deeziz the Unseen moves through the air, entering the oval of orange light. Just before she vanishes, she turns her head towards me. 'Thraxas,' she says. 'You've proved to be rather annoying. I'll see you again, too.'

With that, she vanishes. The orange portal fades, leaving no trace. Our War Leader sits down heavily.

'That woman is impossible to kill,' she gasps. She looks towards her fellow sorcerer, now reclining on her bed. 'Thanks Tirini.'

'You're welcome.' Tirini sits up. 'I feel better.'

'That's because Deeziz was making you sick,' I say.

Tirini Snake Smiter turns to me. Her eyes narrow. 'If I ever hear you repeating that ridiculous story about me being the daughter of a sewer inspector, I'll fry your insides. Magic shoes hiding my background? Absolute nonsense.'

Anumaris Thunderbolt picks up a pair of orange slippers from the floor, beneath the spot where Deeziz disappeared. 'Are these yours?'

Tirini snatches them. 'My normal slippers. What of it? Now if you'll all get out of here and leave me alone, I have some hair and make-up to attend to.'

We withdraw. Makri helps Droo to her feet. Outside the tent, Lisutaris examines the wound in her shoulder. She apologises to the young Elf that she lacks the power to heal her, having used up all her sorcery in the struggle, and sends a messenger to bring a healer. Droo manages to put on a brave face, though I can tell she's quite shocked to have received her first real war wound. Makri and Anumaris are bruised but healthy. I'm feeling healthy enough, though I could do with a beer.

166

'I need to get back to the battlefield,' says Lisutaris.

'Of course. The Generals need you. Congratulations on a fantastic victory. You've probably saved the west. I'll just wait here and—'

'You're coming too, Captain Thraxas. Anumaris, find us some horses. I don't have the strength to get us through the magic space again.'

Chapter Twenty-Two

It's a long time till I'm free to drink beer. The combined armies of the west have just won a notable victory but they're in a chaotic state after the battle. Regiments, phalanxes and battalions are mixed together in confusion. Skirmishers and pursuit troops are still harassing the scattered Orcs, while our baggage and supplies are unprotected in the rear. Lisutaris won't allow this to continue, and issues a stream of orders to her subordinates, bringing things back into order. She could have sent a portion of the army in immediate pursuit of the Orcs but we'd have risked spreading our forces too thinly, probably without dealing another substantial blow. We've won an important victory but we haven't yet won the war. Prince Amrag has plenty of troops at his command. He'll rally his forces. Whether they'll retreat to Turai to fight us there, or regroup to engage with us as we advance, we don't know. We'll find out soon enough. Lisutaris is allowing the army to rest for a day, after which we'll continue our journey east.

'It took courage to march blindly into the clouds like that,' says Gurd, around twelve hours later, when I finally get the chance to sit down at a campfire and fill myself up with stew and beer. 'How did Lisutaris know we'd take the Orcs by surprise?'

'Good judgement. We discussed it. She was hesitant, but I persuaded her.'

I'm sure Lisutaris won't be telling anyone that she advanced on the advice of the High Priestess of the Vitin Oracle. People will assume she gained knowledge of the Orcish position due to some clever piece of magic. It's best to let them think that. Makri appears, looking weary. She's been all over the battlefield and the army camp with Lisutaris. Tanrose ladles food into a bowl and hands it to her.

'A good day,' says Makri. 'Even if I didn't get to fight much.'

'Don't worry,' I tell her. 'We can't all be heroes.'

'You never saw any action either!'

'Makes no difference,' I say. 'I've been a vital part of the war effort. Tracked down Deeziz, protected our War Leader, and generally served as an inspiration to the army.'

'An inspiration?' Makri raises her eyebrows.

'Of course. When Lisutaris was dithering, wondering if she should advance with a bunch of raw, untested troops behind her, she looks at me and thinks "If a warrior like Thraxas is on our side what can go wrong? There's a man who won't let you down."'

Makri shakes her head, and laughs.

'Are all the generals supporting Lisutaris now?' asks Gurd. He was close to the front lines when we mowed down the Orcs, and emerged without a scratch.

'Yes. No one's questioning her leadership.'

We took very few casualties in the battle. The Samsarinans, the Simnians, the Niojans, the Elves, the collected troops from the smaller nations - they all came through almost completely unscathed. It was one of most comprehensive victories ever recorded against the Orcish armies.

'It will make things easier now Lisutaris is secure in her command,' I say.

Makri nods. 'Especially now that Legate Apiroi's out the way.'

'What do you mean?'

'He was killed in the battle.'

'What?' I'm startled by this piece of news. 'Apiroi? Killed? Are you sure?'

'I saw his body.'

I can hardly believe the Legate is dead. We took very few casualties, and he didn't seem like the sort of man to fling himself into danger unnecessarily.

'Surely he wasn't leading the Niojans into combat?'

Makri shrugs. She doesn't know how he met his end, but she's quite certain he's dead.

'Some people always die, even when you win,' says Gurd. 'Just bad luck if it happens to be you.'

I drink some beer and take another helping of Tanrose's excellent stew. I'm still startled by the news of Legate Apiroi's untimely demise. We sit round the fire talking till Tanrose yawns and announces that she needs to sleep. It's now close to dawn and there are faint streaks of daylight on the horizon. I'm tired too. I feel like I've been walking, running or fighting for days on end.

My joints ache as I haul myself to my feet. Makri accompanies me on the walk back to my wagon.

'It was smart of you to identify Deeziz.'

'Maybe Lisutaris will give me a medal.'

'I doubt it.'

'It's just as well you believed me,' I say to Makri. 'No one else did.' If Makri hadn't made the instant decision to attack Saabril, thereby causing her to reveal herself as Deeziz, I don't know if I'd ever have managed to convince Lisutaris. 'She should know to trust me by now.'

'She does trust you, more or less.'

I come to a halt.

'What is it?'

'I don't like it that Legate Apiroi is dead.'

'You don't?' says Makri. 'I thought it was excellent news. He was practically blackmailing Lisutaris. Threatened to tell people she went to the oracle if he didn't get a place on the command council.'

'Remember when Lisutaris told us about that? In my wagon? Didn't you think it was strange that she didn't seem very worried?'

'I didn't notice she wasn't worried. I think she was.'

'She wasn't as worried as she should have been.'

'What are you getting at?' asks Makri.

'You said you saw the Legate's body. Where is it?'

'Laid out with the other Niojan casualties. There weren't many of them. They'll be buried tomorrow.'

'Show me where they are.'

'Have you suddenly lost your reason? We've been running through the magic space fighting trolls, Orcs and sorcerers, and now you want to look at bodies?'

'Yes.'

Makri shrugs. 'I don't like to sleep too much anyway.'

She leads me through the encampment. Though dawn is approaching no one is yet stirring. The troops will be sleeping late today, a rare luxury.

'In that tent.' Makri points towards a large, square canvas construction.

The tent is unguarded. No one sees us as we enter. Inside there are ten bodies laid out carefully on the ground. They're all wrapped in their black cloaks, distinctive garment of the Niojan army. Each has their hands clasped in front of them, resting in death. The Niojans are treating their casualties with respect before they're buried. There's one long table on the room. Lying on the table is Legate Apiroi. He looks peaceful. I stride forward to examine him. There's a deep wound in his throat.

Makri peers at the body. 'That would have killed him instantly.'

'I suppose it would.' I grab the body and turn it over. Doing this requires a lot of strength, and wouldn't count as treating the corpse with due respect.

'What are you doing?'

I study the back of the Legate's brown leather tunic. When he went into battle, he'd have been wearing a solid breastplate, with chainmail covering his back. High-quality chainmail, probably, enough to offer good protection. I bend down to examine him.

'There,' I say, pointing.

'What am I meant to be looking at?'

'That tiny hole in the tunic.'

'What about it?'

I pull the tunic up. Half way up the Legate's spine is a tiny mark, very hard to make out unless you're looking for it.

'You know what that is?'

'No,' says Makri. From the tone of her voice I'm not certain she's telling the truth. Makri is generally a poor liar.

'It's the mark made by an assassin's dart. Small enough to penetrate chainmail, if used by an expert. Poisoned, no doubt. Fired into him under cover of the confusion of battle.'

'An assassin's dart? This is sounding ridiculous.'

I haul the Legate back into his original position. 'Hanama killed him. Presumably on Lisutaris's orders. She brought him down with a dart, removed it, then cut his throat to make it look like he was killed in battle. Smart move by Lisutaris, I suppose. Got rid of the problem.'

'I don't believe it,' says Makri.

'You probably knew about it already.'

171

'No I didn't! I still don't believe it anyway.'

I stare at Makri. 'I hate assassins. Legate Apiroi was an annoying, power-seeking fool but he didn't deserve to be murdered by Hanama.'

'You have no proof he was. Who cares, anyway? We're better off without him.'

'You think so? If Lisutaris did send Hanama to kill him, she probably used sorcery to cover it up. That has a tendency to go wrong. Other people have sorcery too. The Niojans for instance. If they find out about this the trouble will be ten times worse.'

We leave the tent. I'm tired. I feel a strong desire to sleep for a long time. A few Niojan sentries cast unfriendly glances at Makri as we pass through their area of the encampment.

'Lisutaris isn't Queen of the West, you know. She doesn't get to decide who lives or dies.'

'She has to do what's right for the army,' says Makri, stubbornly.

'Assassinating a Niojan diplomat isn't right for the army.'

'I'd say it was.'

'That's hardly a surprise, given your past record.'

Makri halts, and stares at me. 'What do you mean by that?'

'I mean you're no stranger to executing people when you feel like it. Without bothering about the niceties of the law.'

'When did I ever do that?'

'Back in Turai. You killed Rittius, Head of Palace Security.'

'He was a traitor!'

'I *suspected* him of being a traitor. I was about to arrest him when you decided that was too much trouble, and stabbed him instead.'

'I can't believe you're complaining about that! Have you forgotten how many Turanians died outside the city walls when the Orcs attacked? Rittius betrayed the city. You said he poisoned Galwinius as well.'

'I said I suspected he poisoned Galwinius. I'd have liked to see him stand trial for it. But you just decided you'd execute him. No wonder Lisutaris likes you as her bodyguard, you're as bad as each other.'

Makri is furious. She's not a woman who takes criticism well. 'Rittius deserved to die! Turai was besieged, there was never going to be a trial and you know it. And I don't remember you being so upset at the time that I'd got rid of him.'

'I had other things on my mind. Like doing my duty and protecting the city. Not running around killing fellow citizens. Not that you've ever actually been a citizen.'

That's quite a wounding remark. Makri wasn't an official citizen of Turai though she'd made her home there. I feel like wounding her. I'm tired and angry. I'm feeling a strange sense of depression after the elation of defeating the Orcs. I don't like it that Lisutaris sent Hanama to kill Apiroi. It's illegal, and I believe in the law.

Makri regards me with loathing. 'I'd never want to be a citizen of any place you lived.'

'Fine. We weren't looking to recruit homicidal pointy-eared Orcs anyway.'

Makri's hand flies to the pommel of her sword. She controls herself, with an effort. 'I hate you. Never speak to me again.' Makri turns on her heel and marches off.

A few Niojans in the distance are laughing. I catch a snippet of their conversation. Something about a fat Turanian and a crazy Orc woman. Fair enough. I trudge on, heading back to my place in the camp. On the way I pass by the parked wagons under the command of the Simnian Quartermaster Calbeshi. He laughs when he sees me.

'Thraxas, you look worse than usual, and that's saying something. Where have you been? Hiding from the action again?'

'Just give me a beer, Calbeshi.'

The quartermaster fills up a leather tankard and hands it over. The sun is rising in the sky and it's a warm morning. I sit down, rest my back against the quartermaster's wagon, drink my beer, then fall asleep.

Chapter Twenty-Three

A few hours later I wake up feeling refreshed. Calbeshi and his men are nowhere to be seen. Lazing around somewhere, I suppose. Indolent Simnians. I head back towards my unit's wagon. It's a warm afternoon and I might get the chance for some more sleep before we set off tomorrow. I should make sure we're ready to go, but Anumaris will probably take care of it. With the warm sun overhead, I'm feeling almost jovial as I stroll through our encampment. There's not much activity. A few soldiers can be seen, checking their equipment, but most people are taking the opportunity to rest.

As I'm walking past the end of the Turanian section I find myself confronted by Tanrose. She appears to be annoyed. I've no idea why.

'What did you say to Makri?' she demands.

'What?'

'What did you say to her? Why did you upset her?'

'A minor disagreement. Nothing important.'

'Nothing important? I've never seen her so upset.'

'That's hard to believe. She's always upset.'

'Why did you tell her she wasn't welcome in Turai?'

'That's not really an accurate–'

'Didn't she stick up for you when everyone thought you were wrong about Deeziz?'

'Yes, but–'

'It's not good enough Thraxas. I thought you'd got over bullying Makri by now.'

'Bullying? Bullying? Are you insane? I wasn't bullying her! She was insulting me. I was just standing up for myself.'

'By calling her a homicidal pointy-eared Orc?'

'Some harsh words may have been spoken. Look, Tanrose, this isn't the Avenging Axe. We're not safe in our tavern now. We're at war. I can't go around being nice all the time. I have a job to do.'

Tanrose isn't looking any less hostile. 'Does this job involve insulting Makri?'

'Strictly speaking, it doesn't. But the need may arise.'

'You're talking nonsense. I insist you make things up with her.'

'You mean apologise? Certainly not. And I'm not taking her flowers either. This isn't a little girl's birthday party. This is war.'

And with that I depart. I don't care what Tanrose says, I'm not apologising to Makri. I'm still furious that Lisutaris ordered Legate Apiroi's murder and I have a notion that Makri knew all about it. Lisutaris, Makri, Hanama, they were all involved in the Association of Gentlewomen back in Turai; an illicit organisation full of troublemakers. You can't trust any of them. The law has no meaning for people like that.

I march on, my good mood evaporating. I review my conversation with Tanrose, hoping I didn't say anything too insulting. She might ban me from her campfire. I'll never get through this war without her food inside me. Just past Lisutaris's command tent I come to an abrupt halt. Makri, with her back to me, is engaged in conversation with an Elf: See-ath, her ex-lover. Either she's finally decided to confront him, of they've just run into each other accidentally. Either way, Makri isn't comfortable, from the way she's shifting her feet and looking down at the ground.

'I'm sorry about all these messages,' she mumbles.

See-ath regards her unsmilingly. His long blonde hair flows over his shoulders. He's a handsome young Elf. I don't take to him.

'You caused me a lot of trouble,' he says. 'So many messages. The communication sorcerer on Avula told everyone. I was the laughing stock of the island.

Makri shuffles her feet some more. 'I'm sorry I sent them.'

'I'd never have got involved with you if I'd known you were mad. You threatened to chop my head off!'

Makri hangs her head, and doesn't seem to know what to say.

'And now you've been making a fuss again,' continues the Elf. 'Do you think people haven't noticed you diving for cover when I approach our War Leader's tent? Everyone in my unit knows about you. My commanding officer is on the verge of complaining to Lisutaris. Do you have to keep humiliating me? Can't you act normally?'

Makri's head is already hanging in shame. It droops even lower. 'I'm sorry.'

'You were lucky I paid any attention to you in the first place. You know what people said when I started talking to a woman with Orcish blood? They said I'd end up tainted. And they were right. I must have been insane.'

Having now heard enough of this, I stride forward, walk past Makri and grab the front of See-ath's green tunic. Then, using a move I perfected in the schoolyard, I hook his leg and push him over. He falls to the ground, startled. I glare down at him.

'Mind your language when you're talking to Makri,' I tell him. 'You should count yourself lucky she paid you any attention at all, you scrawny excuse for an Elf. You can go tell your unit, your Commander and your whole damn island that Ensign Makri of the Commander's Personal Security Unit, Sorcerers Auxiliary Regiment, bodyguard to our War Leader, undefeated champion gladiator of the Orcish lands, top student at Turai's distinguished Guild College and recent victor in the prestigious Samsarinan sword-fighting tournament, has better things to do that waste her time on you. If I catch you being rude to her again I'll knock your head off.'

I take Makri's arm. 'Let's go.'

Makri allows herself to be led away. Her head and shoulders are still hunched in shame and it takes her a while to come out of it.

'Thanks for rescuing me,' she says, as we arrive at my wagon.

'You're welcome.'

She looks down at my hand. 'You can let go my arm now.'

I release my hold. I notice Makri's eyes are moist. 'Are you going to burst into tears? If so, get in the wagon where no one can see.'

Makri sniffs. 'I'm all right.'

'You'd probably better get in the wagon anyway, just in case.'

The wagon is empty. Makri sits down, dabs her eyes, and recovers her composure. She looks up at me. 'I was planning never to speak to you again. You were very insulting.'

'Only in an inconsiderate, heat-of-the-moment sort of way. Happens all the time between companions at war.'

There's a few moments silence. I really could do with some beer. At that moment Droo clambers in with a smile on her face and a bottle of wine she's filched from somewhere.

'I saw you push See-ath over!' she laughs. 'I never liked him.'

We drink Droo's wine as the day passes, and do little else. Anumaris and Rinderan appear. They've both been satisfactory as security assistants. More than satisfactory, in Anumaris's case. My unit would be in chaos without her organisational skills. I should probably tell her that, in light of all the abuse I've given her. I'll think about it. No point filling her head with praise this early in her military career. I *will* mention her good work to Lisutaris, when I next make a report. It's a more relaxing afternoon than might have been expected, given that we'll be marching east tomorrow. The further we go, the more likely it is that we'll encounter the Orcish dragons. That won't be pleasant. It will bring us closer to Turai however, and Makri and I are both pleased at the thought. When we were chased out of the city I wasn't sure that I'd ever be able to return. Now, after our victory over the Orcs, it seems possible.

Makri falls asleep beside me, her head resting on my shoulder. I reflect on the day's events. I'm still troubled by Apiroi's death. If there was anything suspicious about it, I can see trouble ahead. The Niojans aren't fools. Lisutaris may find herself with some explaining to do. Perhaps I'm worrying unnecessarily. People die on the battlefield. No one else may even suspect there was anything unusual about his demise.

I take a final sip of wine, finishing the bottle. Deeziz the Unseen has been banished from our camp and Captain Thraxas is in good standing with everyone. Not so bad, all things considered. I close my eyes and drift off to sleep beside Makri.

The End

Martin Millar was born in Scotland and now lives in London. He wrote the Thraxas series under the name of Martin Scott. Thraxas won the World Fantasy Award in 2000.

Other Books by Martin Millar

Kink Me Honey
The Goddess of Buttercups and Daisies
The Anxiety of Kalix the Werewolf
Curse of the Wolf Girl
Lonely Werewolf Girl
Suzy, Led Zeppelin and Me
Love and Peace with Melody Paradise
Lux and Alby Sign On and Save the Universe (graphic novel)
Dreams of Sex and Stage Diving
The Good Fairies of New York
Ruby and the Stone Age Diet
Lux the Poet
Milk, Sulphate and Alby Starvation

Printed in Great Britain
by Amazon

82272183R00109